Jennifer stood at the bottom of the double staircase, and Antony immediately picked her out of the milling crowd. No man with a drop of testosterone in his body could miss the magnificent redhead in the sparkling sapphire-blue gown.

Even in his daydreams she hadn't looked this good. And he'd had some wild daydreams about her lately.

He checked his watch. He usually liked making a royal entrance. But not tonight. Tonight, he needed to see Jennifer up close. Needed to learn more about her, what she thought, what she believed in. Needed to feel the small of her back as they danced and dream of what life could have been.

Tonight might be his last chance to enjoy the company of the kind of woman he dreamed he could marry.

And he didn't want to waste a single moment getting started.

Dear Reader,

Celebrate the holidays with Silhouette Romance! We strive to deliver emotional, fast-paced stories that suit your every mood—each and every month. Why not give the gift of love this year by sending your best friends and family members one of our heartwarming books?

Sandra Paul's *The Makeover Takeover* is the latest page-turner in the popular HAVING THE BOSS'S BABY series. In Teresa Southwick's *If You Don't Know by Now*, the third in the DESTINY, TEXAS series, Maggie Benson is shocked when Jack Riley comes back into her life—and their child's!

I'm also excited to announce that this month marks the return of two cherished authors to Silhouette Romance. Gifted at weaving intensely dramatic stories, Laurey Bright once again thrills Romance readers with her VIRGIN BRIDES title, *Marrying Marcus*. Judith McWilliams's charming tale, *The Summer Proposal*, will delight her throngs of devoted fans and have us all yearning for more!

As a special treat, we have two fresh and original royalty-themed stories. In *The Marine & the Princess*, Cathie Linz pits a hardened military man against an impetuous princess. Nicole Burnham's *Going to the Castle* tells of a duty-bound prince who escapes his castle walls and ends up with a beautiful refugee-camp worker.

We promise to deliver more exciting new titles in the coming year. Make it your New Year's resolution to read them all!

Happy reading!

Mary-Theresa Hussey

Mary-Theresa Hussey
Senior Editor

Please address questions and book requests to:
Silhouette Reader Service
U.S.: 3010 Walden Ave., P.O. Box 1325, Buffalo, NY 14269
Canadian: P.O. Box 609, Fort Erie, Ont. L2A 5X3

Going to the Castle

NICOLE BURNHAM

SILHOUETTE *Romance*®

Published by Silhouette Books

America's Publisher of Contemporary Romance

For Doug, my own Prince Charming
and
for Mom and Dad, who never doubted I could do it.
With very special thanks to Tracy Cozzens,
for reading (and rereading!) everything I write,
and to Karen Templeton, for putting in a good word.

 SILHOUETTE BOOKS

ISBN 0-373-19563-X

GOING TO THE CASTLE

Copyright © 2001 by Nicole Burnham Onsi

Visit Silhouette at www.eHarlequin.com

Printed in U.S.A.

NICOLE BURNHAM

is originally from Colorado, but as the daughter of an army dentist, grew up traveling the world. She has skiied the Swiss Alps, snorkeled in the Grenadines and successfully haggled her way through Cairo's Khan al Khalili marketplace.

After obtaining both a law degree and a master's degree in political science, Nicole settled into what she thought would be a long, secure career as an attorney. That long, secure career only lasted a year—she soon found writing romance a more adventuresome career choice than writing stale legal briefs.

When she's not writing, Nicole enjoys relaxing with her family, tending her rose garden and traveling—the more exotic the locale, the better.

Nicole loves to hear from readers. You can reach her at P.O. Box 229, Hopkinton, MA, 01748-0229, or through her Web site at www.NicoleBurnham.com.

Dear Reader,

Most writers say their stories come alive when they ask themselves, "What if?" Stephen King got a case of the "what ifs" while cleaning a woman's locker room. Before long, Carrie scared us all. Agatha Christie speculated about her fellow passengers during an Egyptian cruise. The result was *Death on the Nile,* one of my favorite mysteries.

On June 19, 1999, I relaxed in front of the television to watch England's Prince Edward marry Sophie Rhys-Jones. Since I write for bridal magazines, I considered this work—of a sort. During the commercials, I flipped to a CNN story on the problem of war refugees. Soon I began asking myself, "What if?" What if a refugee-camp worker—maybe even someone who dug latrines—met up with Prince Charming? Could two people from such disparate backgrounds learn from each other? Or would they even give each other a second look?

Before Sophie could say, "I do," I was hard at work—this time, for real. Prince Antony diTalora and Jennifer Allen demanded I tell their story, and rewarded me each day at my keyboard by telling me just what could happen if.

Soon I was happy to learn that *Going to the Castle* was a finalist for the Romance Writers of America's Golden Heart Award, and that Silhouette Books wanted me to share Antony and Jennifer's story with you. Turn off the news and enjoy.

Nicole Burnham

Prologue

Another Birthday Bash For
San Rimini's Crown Prince
At Thirty-Four,
Antony Refuses to Settle Down

THE ROYAL PALACE, SAN RIMINI (AP)—
More than three hundred carefully selected
guests converged on this postage stamp-size
country last night to celebrate Prince Antony
Lorenzo diTalora's thirty-fourth birthday in the
royal palace's Imperial Ballroom.

Conversation throughout the evening focused
not on the prince's planned state visit to China
later this week, but on the fact that Antony is
now the oldest San Riminian crown prince not
to have wed and produced an heir.

Despite the hushed gossip filling the ballroom, the crown prince appeared unconcerned
about finding a bride anytime soon. Recent re-

ports have linked him to Lady Bianca Caratelli, but Antony lived up to his reputation as southern Europe's playboy prince last night, bringing as his date German supermodel Daniela Heit, a descendant of England's Queen Victoria.

Over the course of the evening, the prince was spotted dancing with Lady Bianca numerous times, but he chose to dine with Heit and his sister, Princess Isabella. Heit departed early, claiming an early-morning fitting for an upcoming fashion show. Antony did not seem to mind, however, leaving the ball well after midnight with a group of his sister's friends for an after-hours party at an undisclosed location.

Noticeably absent from the festivities was King Eduardo, fueling rumors that the aging monarch's health is in decline. An official palace statement claims the king was "tending to important matters of state." However, sources close to the royal family fear a relapse of Eduardo's earlier heart trouble and suspect he spent the evening secluded in his palace apartments.

If the latter is true, Prince Antony may not remain the playboy prince much longer. According to several members of the San Riminian nobility, King Eduardo's failing health is forcing him to consider an arranged marriage for his eldest son.

"It makes perfect sense," admits Count Giovanni Alessandro, a longtime friend of the king. "Eduardo places his royal duties above all else, and he believes his primary duty is to ensure the continuation of the diTalora line. If Antony is

not married soon, Eduardo will feel he has
failed the people of San Rimini.''

Antony is said to resist the move.

Chapter One

The latrine threatened to overflow in an hour, tops.

Jennifer Allen leaned on her shovel and drank deeply from her worn canteen. Her arms and back throbbed from an afternoon of heavy digging in the summer heat, and sweat ran into her eyes, making her contacts burn, but she couldn't quit now.

If she and the other volunteers didn't finish the hole for the new latrine soon, the residents of the Haffali refugee camp might opt to use the nearby river to relieve themselves. Unfortunately, the river supplied their only source of clean drinking water.

Jennifer dropped her canteen to the ground, then turned to continue her dusty job. As she raised her shovel to dig, she caught sight of an American network news van making its way down the rough mountainside to the camp and leaned her shovel against the side of the pit.

"Hey, Pia," she pointed out the van to her assistant camp director. "Any idea what that's all about?"

The Rasovo civil war had raged for six months now and few American news agencies had visited the camp, even during the early days of the war when American interest in the displaced Rasovars peaked. With no recent bombing in the area, Jennifer couldn't imagine why journalists picked today to make a surprise visit.

However, if the Rasovo Relief Society, for which she worked, wanted to keep the Haffali camp open for women and children fleeing the fighting, they needed more donations. And even more importantly—she glanced at the long line for the latrine—skilled volunteers willing to travel to Rasovo and pitch in with both hands. Perhaps she could turn the news van's intrusion into an opportunity.

"Oh, shoot," Pia grumbled as she climbed out of the half-completed pit for a better look at the van. "They must've heard that rumor about Prince Antony. Hope they don't mind talking to us while we work."

"Prince Antony? What rumor?" Jennifer couldn't imagine what Europe's hottest tabloid cover boy had to do with the Haffali camp. Other than the fact that both Rasovo and his native San Rimini occupied the northern end of the Balkan peninsula, tucked in the Alps between Slovenia and Italy, she saw no link.

Pia raised an eyebrow. "I didn't tell you? Some of the refugees heard on the radio that Prince Antony is planning to visit the camp tomorrow. They came to me for confirmation, since I'm San Riminian. I never received anything from the palace, though, so I told them it was just a rumor."

Jennifer frowned. Nothing official had crossed her desk, either.

"I'm sure you're right. Prince Antony has hundreds of 'clean' charities elsewhere in Europe to use for his public relations purposes," Jennifer finally replied, alluding to the prince's reputation for making grand gestures to humanitarian organizations for the sole purpose of enhancing his family's public image. "He'd never come here. Why mess a good suit?"

She shook her head, thinking of the grandeur of the San Riminian palace. The Haffali camp stood only five miles from the San Riminian border, and thirty from the royal palace. But the ease of life in San Rimini made it feel a world away from the devastation in Rasovo.

Unfortunately for the residents of Haffali, most San Riminians liked to keep it that way.

A yell went up from some of the refugees who'd spotted the news van. "What do you want to do?" Pia prodded. "We don't have time for this."

Jennifer tucked a stray curl back under her Colorado Rockies cap, then picked up her shovel. "Let's keep digging. By the time the journalists locate me and learn there's no royal visit scheduled, the hole will be finished. Then I can try to talk them into doing a story on the camp itself. Get the word out that we're desperate for more staff."

Pia snorted as she climbed back into the pit to continue shoveling. "Nice thought, Jen, but it won't work. Why cover an overcrowded, depressing refugee camp when your assignment is to splash a few pictures of a filthy-rich, drop-dead-gorgeous Prince Charming across the TV screen?"

Jennifer silently agreed, but vowed to convince the reporters to publicize the need for more relief workers.

Besides, if she remembered the fairy tale correctly, Prince Charming never once got his hands dirty helping Cinderella with her chores.

She needed people willing to pitch in and help. Not Prince Charming.

Prince Antony let out a particularly *un*-royal expletive in his native Italian as his helicopter touched down just inside the Rasovar border. He'd traveled through Rasovo many times prior to the outbreak of hostilities, but didn't remember it reeking of raw sewage. Straining to be heard over the noise of the helicopter, he yelled, "I knew Rasovo had its problems, but…whew! Who would fight over a country that smells so bad?"

Giulio, Antony's longtime pilot, offered the prince a half smile. "It's temporary, Your Highness. I understand they had a problem yesterday with the, uh…facilities. We're downwind right now. It won't be so offensive once you arrive at the camp itself."

Antony nodded, glad his secretary convinced him to wear a casual shirt and khaki pants instead of the tailored suits he usually sported for charity appearances. After the recent spate of fundraising dinners and hospice openings he'd been compelled to attend as part of his royal duties, he'd almost forgotten what it was like to visit an area plagued by overcrowding and poor sanitation. Messy, at best.

He patted his pocket. With any luck, the check he carried for a million San Riminian draema would solve the camp's problems.

He squinted, taking in the Rasovar terrain. The refugee camp sprawled in front of them, straddling the so-called Haffali River, the nearly dried-up stream which gave the refugee camp its name. West and south of the camp, jagged mountains isolated the river valley from the worst of the fighting. To the east and north another set of mountains, lower and more gently sloping, defined the border between Rasovo and San Rimini.

Nearby, two news vans rolled to a stop at the edge of the makeshift landing pad. A Land Rover edged between them, then drove the short distance to the helicopter.

"That's your ride, Your Highness," Giulio nodded when the sport utility vehicle stopped and its door opened. "I'll meet you here in two hours."

"Thank you. That will be more than enough time." Antony unbuckled his seatbelt, then climbed out of the helicopter, stopping short when he noticed the driver of the Land Rover had already crossed the landing pad to meet him.

A *female* driver. For some reason, he hadn't expected a woman to be driving the masculine vehicle. Particularly not such a good-looking woman.

She struck him as outdoorsy. Tomboyish. And definitely American. Her long, curly red hair, similar to Nicole Kidman's, was pulled back into a tight ponytail and stuffed through the back of a Colorado Rockies baseball cap. She sported a dusty denim shirt, a khaki vest, khaki shorts, and, he noted, scraped knees.

Despite her scruffy appearance, he bet she'd look better in a ballgown sashaying about the palace than most of the women he knew. She stood about five foot ten, and her worn outdoor clothing did nothing to hide her athletic curves.

She shook his hand—a nice, firm handshake for a woman—and offered what he assumed was her name, though he didn't catch it. The noise of the helicopter's blades, still slowing to a stop, drowned out whatever she'd said.

Not that her name really mattered. She might be pretty, but she was just his driver.

"Prince Antony," he leaned close, speaking near her ear in English. "I'm thrilled to have the opportunity to see your camp." He forced himself not to close his eyes as he caught a brief whiff of her scent. Clean, natural. Like she'd just showered and skipped the heavy perfumes he'd come to expect on a woman.

She smiled in welcome, a broad grin that nearly made him forget about the dust and odor of the rugged camp. "We're very happy to have you here, though I must say, it's a surprise. The palace only notified us of your visit a couple hours ago." She gestured to the Land Rover. "This way, Your Highness."

He waved to the journalists standing alongside the landing pad as he followed her to the Land Rover. Once seated comfortably in back, he popped open his briefcase and scanned the pages his efficient secretary, Sophie, had handed him earlier. He swore to himself, wishing he'd had more time to review the information on the Rasovo Relief Society.

It wasn't that he hadn't wanted to come. On the contrary, his father, King Eduardo, had drilled it into his head from birth that it was his time-honored duty as San Rimini's crown prince to help out his country's less fortunate neighbors. But he'd been told for months that the Haffali refugee camp wasn't safe, that he couldn't risk a visit.

He'd been stunned when Sophie entered his office yesterday evening, just as he returned from a ten-day state visit to China, and informed him that the fighting in Rasovo had moved to the south. She'd scheduled his trip for the next day, just in case the fighting shifted back. He'd been too exhausted from the flight to read the material she'd prepared.

Hopefully the generous check he carried would help disguise the fact he didn't know what he should about the organization.

He snapped his briefcase shut. Perhaps his beautiful-but-nameless driver could fill him in on the most important details.

"I've been told that the director of the camp is also an American. A Miss Jennifer Allen. Will she be giving me the tour today?"

"That's the plan," the redhead replied, her forehead creasing into a frown as she backed the truck away from the landing pad. "Jennifer Allen will be giving you your tour."

Did she not like Ms. Allen? he wondered. He studied the driver's reflection in the rearview mirror. Her look of concern disappeared so fast he almost believed he'd imagined it. She possessed large, friendly blue eyes, a freckled nose, and a full, sensuous mouth. A mouth he bet smiled often, judging from the tiny laugh lines surrounding it. She didn't seem the type to dislike others without good reason.

Hoping to learn more about the camp director, he noted, "I'm surprised you were sent to the helipad alone. I thought Ms. Allen and the rest of her staff would be here."

The driver shrugged, then glanced over her shoulder at him, once again wowing him with her casual beauty. "Actually, I'm surprised *you* made the trip alone. I assumed I'd also be driving a valet or body-guard."

"I am afraid English is not my native language, so there are often words I do not understand. What is this word—*bodyguard?*"

She nodded, as if remembering he spoke Italian in his day-to-day affairs. "Someone to watch over you. You know, for your safety."

"I see. I do not bring a bodyguard on charity visits."

Her eyes widened. Had he impressed her with his willingness to travel without protection?

"My guess is your charity visits are usually safer than this one."

Okay, maybe not.

She steered the Land Rover off the lefthand side of the dirt road to avoid a ragtag group of refugees making their way into the camp. He grabbed the back of her seat to steady himself as the vehicle bumped through a bank of weeds and mud.

They hit solid ground again, and he let go of her seat to lean toward the window and get a better look at the refugees. Three women, six children, one man. All desperately in need of a bath. All with hungry faces and a hunted look in their eyes. The man pulled a cart behind him, filled with bedding, clothing and a few handwoven baskets stuffed with who-knows-what. Antony hated to think of what they'd endured the last few months.

"I'll admit, this isn't the safest place I've been," he noted once they left the refugees behind. "But I have planned to come for some time now. It's my royal duty to give aid to San Rimini's neighbors. I take that duty quite seriously."

She turned the Land Rover off the road and pulled alongside a battered trailer, which bore a sign designating it as the camp's headquarters. Behind the trailer, hundreds of refugees, many in even worse shape than the group they'd passed on the road, waited in line to approach four folding tables, each manned by a relief worker.

Nearby, a medical tent sported a large red cross on its roof. A mess tent, judging from the line of people with trays waiting to enter, stood lower on the hill. Makeshift shelters constructed primarily of blankets, cardboard and tree branches dotted the hillside near the mess tent.

He let out a deep breath as he took in the scene. Sometimes he forgot how different life could be outside the safe, elegant confines of the royal palace, and away from the polished ceremonies and dinners he often attended.

"It's not exactly like life in San Rimini, is it?" she asked, her voice soft as she put the truck in park.

Was she a mind reader, as well? "It must not be easy for you here. Most people wouldn't choose to spend their time surrounded by so much depression and despair," he commented, again picturing her statuesque figure enveloped in a ballgown, sashaying through the palace's Imperial Ballroom.

Turning in her seat, she replied with a voice full of conviction, "There's nowhere I'd rather be. Helping the Rasovars is a labor of love for those of us staffing the camp. They're wonderful people, as you'll see during the tour."

"Then let's go." He couldn't help but admire her enthusiasm. For a brief moment, he wished his driver would give him the tour instead of Ms. Allen. He found her relaxed attitude refreshing and her genuine affection for the Rasovars downright captivating. He wondered what drove her to choose such a difficult lifestyle. From what little he'd seen of her, she seemed the type able to succeed in any setting.

As he exited the vehicle, an odd sensation coursed through him. Something was off. He looked around for a moment, unable to put a finger on what was wrong with the scene.

Then it clicked. No media. Not a single van had followed them from the landing pad. In fact, no one— not even the group of refugees near the trailer— seemed to notice his arrival.

Nearly a year had passed since he last made a tour of foreign refugee camps, visiting sites throughout the war-torn Balkans and earthquake-ravaged Turkey. He remembered being swamped by people eager to shake hands with a famous visitor in an otherwise depressing place. Banners welcomed him and children delighted in performing traditional songs and dances from their homeland for him.

What had happened this time?

"Didn't the news vans follow us down?" he asked once the driver locked the Land Rover. "I specifically requested that CNN and the San Riminian National News be allowed to accompany me on the tour. Did Ms. Allen have problems with the arrangements?"

"One reporter each from CNN and the San Riminian National News will be joining you at the hospital. The other reporters were asked to wait until we finished going through the hospital to join you on your tour."

"By Ms. Allen?" he demanded. "And they *agreed?*"

She squared her shoulders. "That's right."

He was definitely beginning to wonder about Jennifer Allen, and he hadn't even met the woman yet. He'd double the amount of the check in his pocket if it meant his driver could take him on the tour instead.

"Why on earth did she do that?"

The driver gestured toward the mass of refugees huddled in line behind the trailer. "First, the refugees coming into camp are scared of reporters. They've been running for their lives, sometimes forced to hide in the hills for days before they arrive. They fear their enemies might see them on the news and come after them. Until they've adjusted to life at the camp and realize that they're safe here, it's best to keep them insulated from the press."

"Second," she nodded toward the medical tent, "our hospital is overcrowded. We simply can't accommodate the press. *Ms.* Allen," she stressed the name, "spent a great deal of time this morning convincing the reporters that only the two of them specifically mentioned by you could come through the hospital—and those only out of deference to your wishes. Once the reporters understood our space constraints, they generously agreed to wait until you finished that segment of your tour to join in."

Antony frowned. For a driver, she seemed awfully opinionated about how he, a crown prince, should be treated during his visit. Still, he found her willingness to speak her mind refreshing. And attractive. Most women—and most men for that matter—kept their true feelings hidden in his presence.

"I can understand your difficulty," he replied slowly, trying to piece together the right words in English. "However, I've worked with a number of

these journalists before. They can offer some good
publicity for your cause, and are sensitive to your
need to—''

"Here's the woman I've been waiting for,'' she cut
him off. "Then we'll be ready to start the tour.''

He followed her gaze and saw a short blond woman
jogging up to them from the direction of the mess
tent. She carried a clipboard under one arm, which he
assumed meant she was the infamous camp director.

"Sorry I'm late, Your Highness,'' the blonde apologized in San Riminian-accented Italian as she
crossed the narrow roadway. "I needed to take an
important phone call from our U.S. headquarters. I'd
planned to meet you at the helicopter.''

He extended a hand and flashed her what he hoped
was a winning smile. He needed to convince Ms. Allen to allow the media vans into the compound. Although the main purpose of his visit was to see the
refugee camp and offer financial assistance, he
wanted the San Riminian government, and the royal
family itself, to be shown in a good light—namely,
helping those in need. Since Ms. Allen had obviously
mastered Italian—with a San Riminian accent, no
less—certainly she also knew something of his country and its charitable tradition.

"It's a pleasure to meet you, Ms. Allen.''

The blonde took his hand hesitantly. "It's a pleasure to meet you as well, Your Highness. But I'm
afraid you're confused. I'm Pia Renati, the assistant
camp director. You're acquainted with my cousin,
Viscount Renati, I believe.''

"He's a good friend,'' Antony managed. "So
you're not...?''

"This is Jennifer Allen,'' the blonde switched to

English as she handed the clipboard to his driver. "She's the director of the Haffali refugee camp, and will be taking you on your tour today. We both work for the Rasovo Relief Society, who generously finance the operations of this camp—"

He spun toward his driver. "*You're* Jennifer Allen? You're taking me on the tour?"

He'd wished it in the first place, but not now. Not after he'd made it clear he disagreed with the way she handled the media. And especially not after he'd blown her off as being nothing more than a driver when he hadn't clearly heard her name, then proceeded to ask her questions about herself as if she were a third party.

He made a mental note to be careful what he wished for.

Women with the self-control—not to mention the lithe, stunning figure—of a Jennifer Allen made men do wild things. And as the crown prince of San Rimini, he couldn't afford to do wild things.

"Jennifer Allen," she repeated, her demeanor unruffled despite his gaffe, "I felt it important you meet Ms. Renati since, as a San Riminian citizen, she's used her connections to find temporary homes for many of our refugees in your country."

She thanked her assistant director for the information on the clipboard, then gestured to the medical tent, all business. "Now if you'll accompany me, Your Highness, I'd be happy to show you the camp."

Jennifer tried not to stare as a nerve twitched in the prince's jaw. An argument would come out of his mouth any minute, she knew, and she wasn't sure she'd be able to keep up her calm front much longer.

When Pia had described the prince as drop-dead gorgeous, she'd made the understatement of the year.

Gorgeous didn't even begin to describe Prince Antony. No wonder the journalists waiting at the helipad had been so hot to snap his picture.

Sure, she'd seen Prince Antony on TV during the celebrity segments of the news. And she'd noticed his good looks. Who wouldn't? But she'd never found him mesmerizing enough to keep her from changing the channel to the more hard-core coverage of political events and catastrophes like wars, earthquakes and droughts that affected her day-to-day life as a relief worker.

Seeing Prince Antony in the flesh was another matter altogether.

A flat television screen failed to convey the broadness of his shoulders, the sculpted line of his jaw, the rich texture of his wavy black hair, or the quiet pride and confidence of his walk as he'd approached her on the helipad. He'd let his gaze wander over her with approval, then greeted her with a warm handshake, a twinkle in his pale blue eyes, and a devastating smile that made her insides melt.

Then he'd told her, leaning so close to her that she could breathe in his expensive, regal cologne, how thrilled he was to make the trip.

His sexy Italian accent had capped it. She'd been convinced he didn't care about another woman in the world besides her, or another cause besides the one she championed. She couldn't believe she'd been so mistaken about him or his dedication to charity. He seemed genuinely interested in the Rasovars. That, together with his devastating good looks, made him a nearly irresistible package. She'd almost *swooned,* for crying out loud.

Then he'd forgotten her name.

At that moment, she realized he was no different than the politicians who'd made empty promises of funding and support to her parents during their years helping displaced Vietnamese and Cambodian refugees.

Like those politicians, Prince Antony had been trained all his life to make relief workers feel as if he really cared about what they had to say. In his gut, however, he probably didn't care one iota more than his royal position required.

She chided herself for being drawn in by his charm, then decided to let him go on believing she wasn't Jennifer Allen. Tested him to see how he'd react to the stench, the stream of haggard refugees, and the fact that the media remained on the other side of the camp.

He'd refrained from mentioning the odor emanating from the abandoned latrine. He'd expressed sympathy for the refugees walking alongside the road. Those were points in his favor that initially made her wonder if she'd misjudged him.

But then he'd grown irritated about the lack of immediate media attention, and she concluded she'd been right to doubt him. Prince Antony's self-proclaimed thrill at making the trip to Rasovo related solely to the appearance of reporters who'd salivate over his every move. She wondered if he really knew anything about the refugees themselves.

She glanced up the hill, noticing that several photographers had taken up positions with their cameras aimed toward the camp. Prince Antony followed her gaze, then opened his mouth as if to lobby once more for a closer media presence.

"Your Highness," she cut him off as quickly and politely as she could, "I've organized your tour to last ninety minutes. During the first hour, we'll walk through the camp's facilities. I'll show you all the hard work we do here at Haffali and answer any questions you might have about our mission here. We'll start with the hospital, since I know you want the media to be present for as much of your tour as possible."

She started toward the medical tent, hoping like mad he'd follow her without argument. "The Rasovar children want to make a presentation to you, to thank you for taking the time to visit us. I thought it best to schedule the presentation for the end of your visit, when all the reporters could attend. I've also allowed some time after the presentation for the reporters to ask questions about the camp and your reasons for visiting."

He hesitated, looked once more at the line of photographers near the landing pad, then gestured toward the medical tent. Flashing a conciliatory smile, he said, "Wonderful. Where shall we begin?"

A wave of relief washed through her. *Point one, Jennifer.*

"This is our field hospital," she indicated as they covered the last few paces to the tent. "We have seven doctors on staff. Three from the United States, two from Italy, one from England and one from San Rimini."

She led the prince through the wooden doors of the semipermanent structure, noticing the surprise reflected in his eyes as he scanned the long rows of cots lining the walls.

Jennifer nodded to one of the nurses, who nearly dropped a bedpan when she saw the tall, dark-haired man standing in the doorway. "As you can see, Prince Antony, seven doctors isn't nearly enough to handle the demand. Luckily, we have a couple dozen nurses who have taken on many duties typically reserved for doctors. And those who speak Rasovar serve as translators as much as they do nurses."

"It's a difficult language. I understand very little myself. You were lucky to find fluent speakers to work here." He raised an eyebrow toward the cots. "There must be several hundred patients in this tent," he commented. "You wouldn't know it from the outside."

"Three hundred fifty, with more arriving every day."

The two reporters she'd arranged to have on the tour joined them just inside the door, then she led the group down the first row of cots, introducing the prince to some of the patients. Since she'd told the refugees just yesterday that Prince Antony *wasn't* coming, their mouths dropped open in surprise when he walked up to them, shook their hands, and offered them his best wishes for recovery.

After they made their way through the first row of cots, she held up the curtain that separated the adults from the children's section of the hospital. It always cut her to the quick, seeing so many children injured, many of them too young to understand what had happened to them.

Despite the depressing surroundings, Jennifer couldn't help but grin when she noticed Josef, an eleven-year-old whose father was missing, playing cat's cradle as he lay in his cot. Despite worrying about his father's whereabouts and being injured himself, Josef never failed to keep himself happy. Just two days ago, he'd even made an origami dove for her desk.

"For you. For peace. So we both go home soon, yes?" He'd offered her a heartwarming smile as he made the wish in broken English. She'd fallen hard for the optimistic little boy right then and there.

"Hi Josef," she winked at him as she approached with Prince Antony. In Rasovar, she asked, "How's your leg today? Better?"

He dropped his yarn and nodded, but his gaze locked on the well-known man standing beside her.

She switched to English. "This is Prince Antony. He came to visit the camp today. Would you like to practice your English with him?" Even as she introduced the prince, her heart lifted at the little boy's stunned reaction.

Josef struggled to sit up in bed, but the prince held up a hand to stop him. "Please relax, Josef. I'll sit." He grabbed the chair next to Josef's bed and pulled it close before taking a seat. "How long have you been here?"

"Two weeks," Josef said in a near-whisper, apparently still awed at being visited by royalty. "You come here for me? For to visit *me?*"

"I came to visit everyone." The prince leaned forward and dropped his voice to a conspiratorial whisper, "But especially you."

Josef's eyes widened even further, and one of the reporters snapped a picture. Jennifer wished she owned a camera herself so she could capture the moment for Josef's mother.

The prince looked down at the boy's heavily bandaged leg, then commented, "It must have been difficult getting here with that injury. You're a pretty tough fellow."

Josef nodded and puffed his chest. "Very much tough."

Antony smiled, then grabbed a tattered book from the floor beside Josef's bed. "Is this yours? My nanny often read it to me when I was a child." He opened the book and scanned the pictures on the first page. "Would you like me to read it to you?"

Josef's face lit up, brighter than she'd seen in the two weeks he'd lived at the camp. "Please, yes to read. Thank you!"

When Antony started reading, Jennifer forced herself to steady her knees. His rich baritone voice skimmed over the words of the popular children's book in such a lively, upbeat manner that other children sat up in their cots and listened with interest. He imitated the animals' voices, even crowing like a rooster at the appropriate time. When he finally finished, a round of applause went up from both patients and staff.

If she didn't know better, she'd believe he really did put on the presentation for the sole benefit of the patients, and not for the two reporters leaning in with their cameras and tape recorders. No matter what his motive, the fact that he'd made Josef so happy warmed her to the core.

The prince laughed aloud at the applause, handed the book back to Josef, then wished him a speedy recovery. "In a few months, when you are well again,

I would be honored if you could come to the palace in San Rimini and read it to me.''

Prince Antony looked over his shoulder at Jennifer, his eyes bright with an enthusiasm she hadn't expected from him. Her heart jumped in her chest, despite her efforts to resist the prince's obvious magnetism and charm. "I will leave my secretary's phone number with you. Please call when Josef's leg is healed, and we can arrange a visit.''

He leaned toward her then, and she could swear his sparkling eyes held a challenge.

"Perhaps you could accompany him, Ms. Allen?''

Chapter Two

Jennifer stared. San Rimini's crown prince wanted her to come to the palace?

It couldn't be a real invitation, she rationalized. Just harmless flirting from a man with a knack for it. Polite conversation from a crown prince. She struggled for something equally polite to say in return. "Well…"

"Please to visit?" Josef pleaded with her, his eyes full of hope.

She offered her favorite patient a reassuring smile. She couldn't say no, not to a boy whose family had been ripped apart by a war that wasn't his fault. And certainly not to the prince, whose irresistible blue eyes remained locked on her face.

Still, she didn't want Josef to pin his hopes on a prince who wouldn't follow through on a spur-of-the-moment invitation. Finally, she answered, "We'll see, Josef. You have a lot of healing to do first."

Prince Antony turned back to Josef and mussed the child's dark hair in an affectionate gesture. "You must convince her, Josef. Follow the doctors' instructions, and we shall visit in a few months." He turned to Jennifer. "What is it you Americans say? It's the deal?"

"It's a deal," she corrected as politely as possible.

"Yes, deal!" Josef clapped.

"Then I shall hold you to it," he instructed the little patient. Standing up, he surprised Jennifer once again by taking her arm. "Let's keep going," he urged her along, the heat of his hand on her arm upping her temperature by a couple degrees. "I want to meet as many patients as I can."

As they continued through the rest of the hospital, he shook hands with the staff, offered kind words to those recovering from surgery and to women searching for lost relatives among the injured. He paid particular attention to the children, encouraging them to heal quickly so they could return to school once the fighting ended.

All too soon, they exited the hospital and headed toward the rows of makeshift shelters where the refugees lived. Out in the bright Rasovar sun, the prince withdrew a handkerchief from his pocket and patted his brow, while the two reporters walked ahead to snap photographs of a group of Rasovar children playing kickball in the roadway.

"How do the injured survive the trip here in this heat?" the prince asked. "The nearest Rasovar village is miles away. Over the mountains, even." He stopped walking, his forehead creased in thought. "Josef, for example. It is not possible he walked here on his own, like the group of refugees we passed on the road this morning."

Jennifer blinked. The reporters were gone. The tabloids' favorite playboy actually cared about how the refugees found their way to the camp?

"Many of them do struggle to get here under their own power," she explained. "Some are brought partway in carts, by countrymen who have room to spare amidst their belongings. The Red Cross has a few ambulances in the area, too."

"And Josef? What is his story?" Antony's voice filled with a mix of curiosity and concern that sounded almost genuine to Jennifer. If he'd been raised to make people feel that the royal family cared about them, his training certainly worked.

"A San Riminian Red Cross worker drove him here. She found Josef, his mother, and his two sisters huddled in a ditch at the side of the road near the San Riminian border, hiding from guerrillas. Josef was hit by land mine fragments as they fled their village. His mother couldn't carry him any further, but was afraid to leave him behind to look for help."

"And what of the father?"

"A successful clothing designer. Captured after the rebels burned his shop. We're trying to trace him."

Prince Antony blinked and shook his head. "How terrible for the family."

They began walking again, but as they entered the area where the refugees' dilapidated tents stood he put his hand on her arm, once again sending a jolt of warmth racing through her nerve endings.

"At the end of the tour, would you please remind me to mention Josef to the media? I would like them to be present for his visit to the palace. It will give the public a concrete picture of how the Rasovo Relief Society is helping families recover from the war."

He let go of her arm and withdrew a card from his

pocket, indicating the number Josef should call after
he'd recovered. She studied the thick, embossed paper
for a moment and wondered again if Prince Antony
meant anything he said. Could he really want to show
how relief organizations like hers helped people and
encourage television viewers to take an active part?

Or was the magnetic prince simply media-hungry,
wanting to take every opportunity possible to get reporters to the royal palace? She couldn't tell for sure,
but given his longstanding reputation and the way
he'd acted when she'd told him the media couldn't
follow him on all parts of the tour, she tended to
believe he'd do anything to court the press.

She slipped the card into her front vest pocket.
Even if Prince Antony was a publicity hound, something about his reaction to Josef made her positively
wobbly inside. The prince's visit made Josef feel special, no matter what his motive. And that attracted her
to him even more than when he'd leaned in to talk in
her ear on the helipad, or held her arm as he followed
her through the field hospital.

She took a deep breath. She had to force her personal interest in him aside and do what was right for
the refugees. According to the tabloid headlines, Antony was nothing more than a playboy prince. As op-
posed to her own dating life, which had been practically non-existent since she graduated college and
followed her dream of becoming a relief worker like
her parents, the prince dated scads of women.
Wealthy, high-society women. He spent his father's
money and probably only made these charity visits
because it was expected of him.

Well, if he wanted to use her camp to earn a check-
mark on his to-do list of royal obligations, fine. But

she'd get something more than a temporary hormonal rush in return.

A dream for little Josef. A decent donation from the royal family. And most important of all, attention to the fact that the Haffali camp desperately needed workers.

"Of course I'll remind you," she promised. "But I'd like you to do something for me, as well."

He turned to look at her, his intelligent gaze holding her captive. Struggling to keep herself focused on her job instead of the twinkle in his blue eyes, she asked, "During the question and answer session, would you tell the reporters how important it is for people to come work in Rasovo?"

She extracted a booklet about the Rasovo Relief Society from her vest pocket and handed it to him before she could second-guess her boldness. "We're setting up a toll-free number this afternoon to answer people's questions about our organization and to accept staff applications. If you could encourage people to call us, it will go a long way toward helping families like Josef's recover from the war."

"That's it?" his gaze turned quizzical. "A plea for more workers? I assumed your most pressing need would be for donations."

"Donations do help," she admitted. "Immensely. But right now we're desperate for warm bodies. Staff willing to pitch in with both hands and dig latrines, set up tents, feed the hungry, tend to the injured..."

She swallowed, hoping he would understand what she needed to say. "This may come out the wrong way, Your Highness, but donations can only do so much for an organization like ours. I know people mean well when they give us their money. But all the money in the world can't get our patients the medicine they need, for instance, when there aren't enough skilled people here to administer it to them. You're the first official visitor we've had since the camp opened. If people don't care about the plight of the Rasovars enough to visit us, then we certainly can't get them to come work here, no matter how much we can afford to pay them.''

She gestured to the new latrine, now standing over the hole she and Pia had labored on. ''Two of us spent three hours yesterday afternoon in that dirt, digging as hard and fast as we could. But with our staff stretched so thin, we couldn't get the new latrine operational in time to prevent an overflow at the old one. Everyone on the staff, from the doctors right on down to the mess tent workers, could tell you similar stories. There just aren't enough hands.''

''That's why I came,'' his mouth creased into a warm, I'm-here-to-help-you smile. ''I want to personally do all I can to help San Rimini's neighbors here in Rasovo.'' Antony reached into his vest pocket and pulled out a folded piece of paper.

Grateful, Jennifer handed him her pen so he could jot down the Society's new telephone number. ''Thank you, Your Highness. We need all the staff members we can get. Sometimes it seems all we get are checks from people who don't really care, people who just want the problem to quietly go away, but who don't realize that the money means nothing if…''

She clamped her mouth shut, knowing her desire to help the Rasovars led her to make inappropriate statements. Inwardly, she prayed he hadn't been offended by what she'd said, then tried to continue on a more positive note. "What you're doing will help people around the world learn to care, help them see why our mission is important. Actions like yours, speaking for us on the importance of pitching in and working to solve the problem, are more meaningful than any check."

The lines between Antony's eyes deepened into a frown, causing Jennifer to chastise herself for her careless words. Better to just shut up and give him the phone number. He took the pen she offered.

"Within the United States, it's one, eight hundred…"

He scribbled the number on the piece of paper, as well as the number for the Society's European headquarters, then shoved it back into one of the pockets on his khaki vest.

"I'll do what I can. Shall we continue the tour?"

"Of course. The journalists are waiting to accompany us," she gestured past two clotheslines weighed down by hospital linens to the waiting vans.

Once the reporters joined them, she led the group in a circle through the camp, not making any attempts to steer them clear of the dirtiest, most crowded areas. She wanted the prince—and the world—to understand the true desperation of the Rasovars. To see the hardships they were forced to endure. To see the potential in their faces. To see how just a little bit of help could make all the difference in their lives. Perhaps then they'd realize the importance of her call for additional staff.

Finally, the group arrived back at the mess tent, where the children waited to share their presentation and Prince Antony offered to answer the reporters' questions. True to his word, he took the first question as an opportunity to speak about the need for additional staff at the camp. "The number to call is toll-free—" he began.

"Will you be volunteering?" one of the reporters interrupted. The prince shook his head. "I wish I could. Unfortunately my schedule does not allow it."

"What about Lady Bianca Caratelli?" another reporter joked, referring to a woman Jennifer knew to be one of San Rimini's most eligible aristocrats. The group broke out in laughter. Even the prince joined in.

"Are you still seeing Lady Bianca?" one of the more brazen tabloid reporters called out, "Or is there another young lady we should know about?"

"Like Daniela Heit!" another voice chimed in from the crowd.

He was seeing Lady Bianca Caratelli? *And* Daniela Heit? Obviously, working in Rasovo had left her clueless about the social goings-on in the world.

An American reporter standing near Jennifer muttered to his cameraman in a voice loud enough for Jennifer to hear, "Man, I don't know why he felt the need to come down here. This place is a hellhole. We can't even get a decent meal."

"I gotta sandwich in the truck. You want half?"

"Nah," the reporter replied. "We'll be back to San Rimini soon enough. The prince has some fancy dinner to attend tonight, and I bet he's not planning to go alone. He must want out of here as bad as we do."

Jennifer's throat clenched as a wave of disappointment washed through her. Not because the prince garnered so much female attention, though that bothered her more than it should, but because the reporters could care less about the camp. They just wanted to catch the prince off guard in hopes of getting a little royal gossip.

Worse still, the prince hadn't even been able to give out the Society's toll-free number. So much for her dreams of applicants flocking to the phone line. She turned away so no one would notice her frustration. Heck, they'd probably think her grim look meant she was jealous of Lady Bianca or what's-her-name Heit.

A nurse entered the side door to the tent, wheeling Josef in front of her. The boy's eyes filled with excitement when he saw first her, and then the prince.

He tugged on Jennifer's arm, then pointed to his bandaged leg. "See, Miss Jennifer," he yelled up to her so she could hear him over the din of the reporters. "I better! I go in wheeled-chair! We can visit prince soon, yes?"

Jennifer's heart sank right to the dirt floor. She couldn't stand to crush Josef's dreams, even as her own were being trodden by the reporters' ridiculous questions.

Just then, the prince glanced at her over the reporters' heads. His gaze locked with hers, and she wondered what had caused him to look her way.

He winked at her then, surprising her so much she wondered if she'd imagined it. A royal prince, winking at *her?* He turned his gaze down then, grinning at Josef beside her. After giving the little boy's bandaged leg a pointed look, as if to say, "get better," he focused once again on the journalists long enough to give them the Society's phone number.

"Maybe, Josef," Jennifer replied, her heart lifting a little as the prince began to talk about the importance of relief work to Rasovo and its citizens, "Maybe we will."

Prince Antony's limousine eased through the wrought-iron gates of the San Riminian royal palace, then circled to a secluded set of heavy oak doors where Sophie awaited his arrival.

Antony exhaled as the limo eased to a stop and wished he could linger in the plush back seat a while longer. What he wouldn't give to spend just a little more time with Jennifer Allen, learning more about her, about what she did, and perhaps most important, why she did it. Though she was a bit brash for his taste, she had a passion about her work and the people she protected he'd never experienced himself, despite spending a lifetime contributing to charity.

Even more perplexing was the fact Jennifer didn't seem to want or expect his money. She only asked him to speak well of her organization, notifying the media of its desperate need for volunteers. Other charity directors and fundraising chairpersons expected more from him. Some even looked disappointed when he handed them checks that weren't for the exorbitant amounts they'd dreamed of.

He knew he should be thrilled with the outcome of the visit. The check in his pocket could just as well be given to the Red Cross, the San Riminian Cancer Council, or some other worthy cause if the Rasovo Relief Society didn't have an immediate need for it. It could still serve a good purpose.

But he wasn't thrilled. Quite the opposite.

As he'd walked through the camp with Jennifer, listening to her melodic voice try to put a positive spin on the constant threat of floods and disease, and noticing how the refugees smiled at her from their nearly uninhabitable tents, he found himself wanting to do everything and anything in his power to help. And not just to help the refugees.

He wanted to make things better for her.

Why, when the woman seemed to want so little from him, he didn't know.

Still, during the flight home, he'd turned the problem over in his mind, trying to find a solution. He found himself brainstorming ways to keep Jennifer from wearing herself out digging latrines in the hot sun. Using his name and position to recruit the medical personnel necessary to alleviate the worry lines he'd seen crease her forehead when she noticed a doctor take an extra shift. Acquiring food, blankets and vaccines so she didn't have to explain their absence to the refugees who looked to her for everything. Raising the camp's standard of living until the optimistic wishes of her heart came true.

He slammed his hand against the limousine's plush armrest. He'd always been of the opinion that money could buy just about anything, but today, for the first time in his life, he began to realize that it couldn't. As Jennifer insisted, people had to care enough first.

By the time he'd landed in San Rimini, he concluded that what Jennifer meant—though she'd never say it—was that *he* didn't care enough. Perhaps living up to his royal duty meant not only giving out checks, but giving of his heart. Just like Jennifer did.

The revelation shook him to the core. But even more alarming, he wondered how, after hundreds of meetings with relief workers over the years, this woman managed to get under his skin.

Sophie offered him a polite nod as he exited the

limousine and approached the palace doors, then handed him his electronic organizer. Her Italian tinged with a crisp British accent, she stated, "You'll find a new item on the agenda for the evening, Your Highness. Your father has requested you join him in his private quarters as soon as you're refreshed from your flight."

"In other words, immediately."

Sophie did a poor job of hiding her grin. His polished British secretary understood King Eduardo's mind better than he did at times. "He did stress that he needed to see you before your dinner engagement. However, I'm certain he'll understand if you need, say, half an hour?"

He'd forgotten all about his promise to dine with Lady Bianca. He'd need to find some way out of it. After spending the day in Rasovo, he had no desire to listen to Lady Bianca's endless chatter about who was sleeping with whom among San Rimini's social elite. Perhaps his father would provide him the necessary diversion.

"Did my father mention the purpose of this meeting?"

"No, but from his demeanor I'd wager it's Topic Number Six."

Antony bit back a groan. In the parlance he and Sophie worked out years ago to describe King Eduardo's favorite lectures, Topic Number Six meant Antony would soon get an earful on "Royal Duty Supersedes Personal Desires." Just what he needed after spending a day attending to royal duty. And ignoring his desire for a certain scruffy redhead with no royal blood whatsoever.

He punched a couple buttons on his electronic organizer, then asked, "The long version or the short version, do you think?"

"I wouldn't care to guess this time."

"Hmmm. Has Federico had an audience with the king today?" Meetings with Antony's near-perfect younger brother, who'd already married and produced two male heirs to the diTalora line, usually sparked King Eduardo's desire to discuss Topic Number Six.

"I believe they lunched together."

"I see. It will be the long version, then. Thank you, Sophie. I would appreciate it if you could call Lady Bianca and reschedule our dinner. I could be late, and I fear I will not make good company afterward. Besides, with all this travel, I should get some rest tonight."

She gave him a curt, businesslike nod, then turned to walk back to her office.

"Oh, Sophie? I wanted to mention..."

She spun around. "Your Highness?"

"If I receive any further requests to visit the Haffali camp, will you discuss them with me before scheduling?"

Her forehead creased. "I apologize. I understand Ms. Allen wasn't fully prepared for your visit due to a miscommunication. Two hours was too long, Your Highness?"

"On the contrary. I was unable to observe nearly as much as I wanted."

She studied his face for a moment, then her eyebrows rose a notch. "I see."

Twenty minutes later, Antony strolled into the sitting area of his father's private wing. He took a deep breath, struck by the contrast between the royal family's opulent chambers and the makeshift living quarters he'd toured in Rasovo just a few hours earlier. He ran a hand over the gold frame of a well-known Renaissance painting, one of dozens hanging in King Eduardo's living quarters.

The price of just one of the paintings could feed the Rasovar refugees for a month.

Or could it? he wondered. Just because there was money for food, did that necessarily mean that people would be willing to transport it, or prepare it?

And if that was true, did the other difficult problems of the world simply require more volunteers willing to tackle them in order to be solved? That seemed to be Jennifer's logic. He stared at the painting, wishing he'd had another hour or two to pick her brain.

A deep, commanding voice cut through the oak-paneled room, yanking his thoughts away from the redheaded relief worker. "Have a seat, Antony."

Antony's father entered the sitting area, followed closely by a butler who shut the door to the king's bedchamber behind him. The king took his time walking across the room, then sat stick-straight in his favorite leather reading chair, a gift from the queen of the Netherlands. Walking past the matching seat given to his late mother, Queen Aletta, Antony chose instead to sit on a velvet sofa situated across the antique coffee table from his father.

Given the deep frown lines crisscrossing the king's forehead, together with the prescription bottle of heart medication sitting next to his father's crystal water tumbler on the tea tray, Antony figured he'd need all the space he could get.

He was definitely in for the long version of Topic Number Six.

"I understand your trip to China was a tremendous success, my son. I hope you fared as well on your trip to Rasovo today," the king looked over his glasses at Antony. "I take it the Society will make good use of our donation?"

Guilt washed through Antony. He ran a hand over his pocket, which still contained the generous check, only now with the Society's number scrawled on the reverse side. Careful to select the right words, he answered, "They have several viable projects in the works, primarily designed to draw in more workers."

"Glad to hear—" The king shifted in his chair, grimacing as he did so.

The Haffali camp—and its beautiful director—suddenly didn't seem as troublesome to Antony. During his absence in China, then in Rasovo, the king's health had obviously deteriorated. He looked far worse than he did just a few weeks ago, when he'd opted to skip Antony's birthday celebration.

"Are you feeling well, Father?" Antony asked in a low voice.

King Eduardo nodded to his butler, discreetly waiting in the corner. The butler took the tea tray, and the medication with it, then left the room, pulling the heavy oak double doors closed behind him.

Once father and son were alone, the king's rigid posture gave way to a semislump, the formality of his office draining away before Antony's eyes to reveal a tired, sick man, despite the fact his father was only fifty-four.

The king coughed a few times, then managed, "I've taken so many pills the last two weeks I'm afraid I've depleted the royal pharmacy. I can't hide my heart condition from the staff much longer, let alone from the public.''

So it wasn't Topic Number Six after all. Instead, they were to discuss The Special Topic, the topic even Sophie didn't know about. ''The King Has A Heart Condition.''

He preferred to discuss Topic Number Six.

''What'd the doctor say?''

''I need bypass surgery next week. I can't delay it any longer.''

Their gazes locked across the coffee table, each of them reading the silent message in the other's eyes. The surgery involved risk that neither of them cared to consider aloud. Even worse, the tabloids would certainly find out about the king's condition, no matter how hard they tried to keep the surgery quiet.

''Will the doctor be able to clear the blockages?''

''Not entirely. Surgery is only delaying the inevitable.'' The king's eyes clouded for a brief moment. ''I'm afraid I have the same heart problems as your grandfather, my son. My body is aging before my mind is ready to let go.''

Antony let out a deep breath, unaware he'd even been holding it. His grandfather, King Alberto, had died of heart failure when he was only fifty-eight. ''I see.''

King Eduardo stood, and Antony waited while his father paced the room, one slow step at a time. Finally, the king stopped and turned to face him, his expression once again that of a proud, stoic ruler. ''Which is why I've asked you to come. I've impressed upon you since you were very young that your duties as a member of the diTalora family, and as heir to the San Riminian throne, must supersede your personal desires.''

So it was to be Topic Number Six, after all. "Of course.''

"Your primary duty is to provide an heir to the throne. Quite obviously, you must be married to do that.''

"Father?''

The king stopped pacing and held up a hand. "Let me finish. I have urged you to take your time, date as many potential mates as possible. Even arranged dates through some of my titled friends. I've held my tongue about the fact that Federico married and produced heirs, as was his duty, yet you still have not met the 'right woman to be queen,' as you describe her. Unfortunately, I can hold my tongue no longer.''

He ran his fingers through his thick, graying hair. As he dropped his hand back to his side, Antony noticed it shook.

"The way things stand now, I might not survive to see the country's thousandth anniversary celebration next year,'' the king continued. "Therefore, I must concern myself with the dire question of my own succession whether I wish to or not. It is my royal duty.''

Antony nodded his understanding. Over the years, he and his father shared many discussions on what it meant to be a good king to the people of San Rimini. And carrying on the 1,000-year-old diTalora line with its proud traditions served to stabilize San Riminian politics. "I understand the urgency you must feel. But please know, I do plan to produce heirs.''

He shook his head, hating to bring up the topic that really bothered him. "Father, all this dating you have arranged—though I know it is for a good purpose—

has given me a rather nasty reputation in the tabloids.
They've started calling me the playboy prince, and I
despise it. In fact, now that I think about it, when I
met with workers at the camp in Rasovo today, they
seemed to be surprised that I came at all. My guess
is that my new 'reputation' preceded me." He swung
his arm wide. "The last thing I wish to do now is
date another woman, one I know would never make
a good queen for me."

"A good marriage will cure a poor reputation, especially if you do so before taking the throne." The
king returned to his leather chair, leaned forward, and
fixed his gaze on Antony. "You have one year from
today to find and marry a fit bride. Someone of noble
birth who understands what it means to be a diTalora
queen. Someone who will uphold our country's honorable principles of freedom and charity, as your late
mother did. Someone who will produce heirs as soon
as possible after the marriage."

The king coughed a few times, pressed his hand to
his chest, then continued, "You should reconsider
Lady Bianca. I suspect you were not planning to date
her any longer, but I believe she'd make an excel-
lent queen. If you object, Count Alessandro's eldest
daughter would be acceptable, as well."

"Alessandro's daughter is twelve years younger
than I am. Hardly a good match."

"Perhaps." The king shrugged, but remained determined. "There's always Daniela Heit. Though I do
not approve of that modeling business, she has royal
blood, and I understand she has a real appreciation
for our culture. Still, Lady Bianca would be my first
choice. She gives generously to the San Riminian Red
Cross, and she's honorary chair of the San Rimini

AIDS Council. The people would love that. Plus, her bloodlines are impeccable.''

Antony's mind spun as his father continued to reel off the names of eligible women belonging to Europe's most aristocratic families. The tone of the king's voice left no doubt he meant what he said.

Antony rose from the sofa and strode to the opposite side of the room. He understood that his father wanted him to marry and produce heirs, but within a year? How could he possibly find a woman fit to be queen, yet who also loved him for himself, rather than as a prince? He couldn't possibly spend his life in a loveless marriage with a woman who wanted nothing more than his money or the royal title that the marriage would give her. Frankly, he found women like Jennifer Allen—interesting women who were unafraid to speak their mind in his presence—far more attractive.

He gritted his teeth, wishing he could act like a commoner might and punch a hole through the wall, his temper and frustration raged so hot. Schooling himself to keep his countenance calm, he argued, "With all due respect father, how do you expect me to—"

"If you do not, Antony," the king ignored his protest, "you will relinquish your title as crown prince to your brother Federico."

Antony spun around, his control faltering. "You can't do that."

"I can and I will."

"You'd need approval of the San Riminian parliament."

"I already have it."

The king rose and walked toward his bedchamber,

his shoulders hunched as if physically weighed down by the burden of the discussion. "The head of parliament's Succession Committee joined me for dinner last week, while you were in China. He specifically asked me if you planned to marry anytime soon. When I told him he would be the first to hear of any impending nuptials, he made it clear that Federico is also an acceptable choice to the Committee to succeed me on the throne."

Antony frowned. Only twice in the thousand-year history of the diTalora line had a second son been permitted to take the throne. It wasn't unprecedented under San Riminian law for the Succession Committee to consider Federico in his place, given the fact that Antony hadn't yet produced an heir, but it was an unusual move.

"Has the Committee heard something about your heart?" Antony asked. "My coronation as crown prince took place six years ago, with the Committee's unanimous approval. Why should they believe succession is even an issue?"

"I said nothing of my poor health, but there have been rumors circulating for almost a year, ever since I quit taking my daily jogs through the city's parks. The tabloids have even been speculating as of late. Certainly long enough for the Committee to reconsider your place in the royal line." The king shook his head as he continued to pace the large, oak-paneled room. "When the tabloids get wind of my surgery next week, I guarantee the Committee will actively push to put Federico on the throne. Federico has two sons, ensuring that the diTalora line will continue. Princess Lucrezia has stated publicly that she hopes to give Federico a third child soon. You offer San Rimini no such assurances.''

''You want to reassure the people by preventing me from ruling, though I've spent a lifetime formulating a plan of action for our long-term economic benefit?'' He swung his arms wide. ''Federico has made no such plans, has no idea how to move the country into the modern age along with the rest of Europe. And he certainly isn't prepared as I am to attend to the more delicate matters of state. He has far less experience as a diplomat.''

Antony stared at his father, hardly believing the turn of events. ''Rather than leading them as I've been trained to do, you want me to reassure our people by entering a loveless marriage that could divide the country, as the Charles and Diana scandal divided England?'' Or, he thought, a loveless marriage like Federico's, a marriage with problems kept secret from those outside the royal family.

''Of course I'd prefer you to marry a woman you love, but my primary duty is to ensure that the di-Talora line continues after my death. I do not doubt your abilities as a king, or the foresight you've shown in planning for the future of our country. However, without a son of your own to continue your ambitious work, I have no choice.''

The king opened the door to his bedchamber, then pulled the thick velvet cord hanging above the light switch to summon his valet. ''I'm sorry, my son. You have no choice, either. You must marry within a year.''

Chapter Three

Sophie cleared her throat, jogging Antony's focus from the brochure he'd been reading on the Rasovo Relief Society.

"I'm sorry, Sophie," he apologized, straightening in his desk chair. "I suppose I'm a bit distracted this morning."

She nodded to the stack of law books on his centuries-old French mahogany desk. "Something I can research for you, Your Highness?"

He shoved back from his desk, the antique chair creaking as he did so, and stood to stretch. "No, Sophie, but thank you."

He'd been reading nearly all night, yet every law book and history text he scoured led him to the same conclusion. The Succession Committee would be well within its rights to strip him of his title as crown prince and give the honor to Federico. He doubted even Sophie could find him an escape. Frustrated by the texts, he'd turned to reading the Rasovo Relief

Society brochure, which he found far more interesting.

Reluctantly, he shoved the brochure into his desk drawer, then buttoned the front of his double-breasted suit and adjusted his sterling-silver cufflinks. "I take it you're here to review my agenda for the day?"

"Of course." She punched a few buttons on the electronic organizer she never seemed to be without. "Your barber will be here for your haircut in a half hour. Then the luncheon for the San Rimini Historical Society is at eleven. Finally, you'll be meeting with the economic council at two, at which time they'll update you on the progress being made on our new trade agreements with Italy. The meeting is scheduled to last two hours."

"Fine." He jumped on the topic, anxious to wrap his mind around something besides thoughts of Jennifer Allen. "I'm eager to hear their opinions regarding my latest proposals."

Sophie tapped the organizer's keypad a few more times, then looked up at him, as if startled. "I almost forgot, Your Highness. Lady Bianca Caratelli called last night while you were meeting with your father. I assume she wished to reschedule dinner."

"Most likely."

"Well, I wanted to speak with you first, but your father approached me this morning to see if there was space in your schedule to dine with Lady Bianca this weekend. He was quite adamant about squeezing her in. I know you mentioned sponsoring a dinner on Friday to kick off your new San Riminian Scholarship Fund, but I wasn't aware—"

"The old man certainly is determined." Antony's temper flared anew. Sophie's eyes widened at his unusual outburst, and he held up a hand to reassure her. "It's all right, Sophie, it's just…"

An idea struck him with such force he sat back down in his desk chair. Perhaps, just perhaps, he could kill two birds with one stone.

"You mentioned the San Riminian Scholarship Fund dinner. It's on Friday?"

"Yes, Your Highness. As you requested, it's scheduled in the Imperial Ballroom at 8:00 p.m. Approximately four hundred guests have confirmed."

"Good," he aimlessly ran his hand along the top of the desk, his mind working overtime. "Have the requirements for earning a scholarship been made public yet?"

"Not to my knowledge. We've only sent out the press release regarding the founding of the scholarship fund itself."

"Good. Because I'm about to add a service requirement."

With any luck, he'd prove to himself and to Jennifer Allen that he could do far more than just write checks to help a cause. He'd show he cared about her organization and what they stood for. And he'd get her the help she so desperately needed.

Plus, with Lady Bianca in attendance, he'd quiet his father's, not to mention the Succession Committee's, fears concerning his future. He smacked his hand against the desk hard enough to make Sophie jump, thrilled as the pieces of his plan snapped into place. If he played his cards right, perhaps he'd even convince his father to revoke his absurd ultimatum.

"Arrange for Lady Bianca to attend the scholarship dinner. Seat her on the dais next to me." He pulled the Rasovo Relief Society's contact information from his desk drawer and handed it to Sophie. "Then see if you can get a call through to Jennifer Allen at the Haffali refugee camp. It's important I speak with her as soon as possible."

Sophie perused the brochure, her face breaking into the same amused look she'd had the day before, when he'd told her about his visit to Rasovo. "I understand perfectly, Your Highness."

"*This* Friday? Your Highness, I'm truly honored, but I'm needed here at the camp." Jennifer's hand shook as she held the telephone. She could hardly believe Prince Antony had called her, especially after the way she'd yammered at him during his visit. And with an invitation to a private fundraising dinner, to boot.

Tempting, she had to admit. Who wouldn't want to attend a fancy soiree with a gorgeous prince? Especially since she hadn't been out on the town with a man—romantically or otherwise—since before she graduated college and immersed herself in her relief work.

But the trip would be impossible. The Rasovars' interests had to come first, just as they had done on the occasions she'd been asked out by the journalists or Red Cross workers who'd traveled through the camp. She needed to stay put.

"Besides," she fumbled for something to lighten the conversation, "I couldn't possibly find a dress in time. I don't exactly have a closetful of formal wear with me at Haffali."

Antony laughed at her feeble humor, a deep, rich laugh with substance she hadn't expected from him.

A laugh that made her stomach tighten with desire. What was it about this man that made her so loopy?

"Before you say no," he replied, "let me explain a little about the scholarships—and about why I need you at the dinner."

Jennifer frowned. What did the San Riminian Scholarship Fund have to do with her?

Antony continued, not allowing her the chance to dissuade him. "I recently created the scholarship fund to help San Riminian students finance their college studies. Applicants must show financial need and have an outstanding academic record."

"I'm sure it will help a lot of students, Your Highness."

"I hope so. But something you said yesterday made me think. Do you remember when you mentioned that money alone couldn't solve the world's problems?"

Jennifer rolled her eyes. Why couldn't she keep her big mouth shut? "I apologize for that, Your Highness. I—"

"Please, do not apologize," he interrupted. "What you said made me realize that the San Riminian Scholarship Fund could be used to help the Rasovars."

"Really?" She couldn't imagine how.

"I'd like to incorporate a service requirement. Anyone who receives a college scholarship must spend their summers working for a charitable organization, such as the Rasovo Relief Society."

Jennifer slumped back into her desk chair. Could he be serious? From what Pia had told her, Antony's scholarship fund would support nearly fifty students a year. If even ten of them came to work for the Rasovar Relief Society...

"Ms. Allen?" the prince's smooth, regal Italian accent cut through her thoughts, "I hope you approve?"

"Of course I do!" she managed. "The extra staff would be a godsend to us. I don't know how to thank you."

"By coming to the fundraising dinner and speaking about your organization and its needs."

Jennifer straightened. If her presence at the dinner brought as much attention to the refugees as the prince promised, the rest of the staff would certainly cover for her for a day or two. Maybe attending wasn't so impossible. But to actually pull it off?

"I'm not sure how I'd get there—"

"I'll send my pilot. Would noon on Friday be acceptable?"

"Noon Friday is fine, but—"

"Wonderful!"

"But...well, there's still the problem of finding a suitable evening dress. They don't exactly carry them in Rasovo's shops these days."

"Not a problem. My secretary, Sophie, will take your sizing information and have a selection of gowns available for you upon your arrival. I'll see you on Friday."

"Really, you don't need to..." Jennifer got out, then realized he'd already handed the telephone to Sophie. She reluctantly gave her measurements to the prince's secretary, then hung up the phone, stunned by the conversation she'd just had.

Glancing out her trailer window, she noticed storm clouds moving in over the mountains. A refugee walking along the path nearby pulled up her collar against the wind, studied the darkening sky, then turned and headed into the relative comfort of the mess tent. Come morning, Jennifer knew the camp would be a soggy, muddy mess.

She watched the tent door swinging in the wind, then shook her head. She had to forget about her stupid, schoolgirl attraction to the prince. *Had to.*

Friday night, she'd get a once-in-a-lifetime opportunity to tell the world about the cause dearest to her heart. If a handsome prince happened to lend her a ballgown and dine with her at the same time, then so be it. Her focus would remain firmly on the refugees and their needs. Not on a tall, dark and handsome Prince Charming. Not if he leaned in to whisper in her ear again. Not if he touched her arm again. Not even if he asked her to dance in that incredible Italian voice of his.

Whipping a pad of paper from her desk drawer, she forced herself to concentrate on the speech she needed to write. Her parents spent years speaking out for Vietnamese and Cambodian refugees, garnering barely enough support for subsistence. However, they'd never been presented with the kind of opportunity Prince Antony was offering.

"Maybe," she mumbled to herself, "maybe he *is* different from the others." After all, he'd read to Josef with such heart, and then he'd come through with a plan to bring her more volunteers—a plan she had to admit was impressive—how could he possibly be like all those other politicians?

Aside from the fact he was far, far sexier, of course.

She smiled as she put pen to paper. Maybe, just maybe this time, she could succeed where her parents' efforts failed. And she could do it with Antony's help.

* * *

Jennifer made herself sit ramrod-straight on the edge of the sitting room's red silk jacquard sofa. Somehow, maintaining anything less than perfect posture as she awaited the prince's secretary felt wrong. The austere palace setting demanded it.

She glanced at her watch for the third time since entering the room, then, frustrated at the slow passage of time, turned her attention to the ceiling. The chandelier dripped with crystal. Above it, an ornate scene had been painted across the ceiling to make it look as if the heavens had parted to allow a group of cherubs to hold the ornate chandelier aloft.

Swallowing hard, Jennifer looked back down at her less than regal clothes, then brushed a hand across her linen pants. Thank goodness the prince's secretary would be meeting her instead of the prince himself. If he saw how underdressed she was for a visit to the palace, he might reconsider his offer.

"Ms. Allen?"

Jennifer jumped in her seat. The heavy wooden doors swung so quietly across the plush oriental rugs, she hadn't heard the secretary's entrance. The middle-aged woman's tweed suit and clipped British English would have made her consider running for the exit, were it not for the warm, friendly smile on her face.

"Yes?" Jennifer squeaked out once her nerves settled.

"I'm Sophie Hunt, Prince Antony's private secretary. Please feel free to call me Sophie." She crossed the room and offered her hand. "I trust Giulio made the trip a pleasant one?"

Jennifer rose and shook Sophie's hand. "I admit, I was nervous about flying in a helicopter. I've never been in one before. Giulio made me feel quite comfortable, though.''

Sophie nodded. ''Glad you enjoyed it. Now, if you will come with me, we only have a few hours before the dinner.''

Jennifer followed as Sophie led the way out of the sitting room and through a series of marble hallways, her smart heels click-clacking against the cold, polished floors. Mirrors trimmed in gold covered the walls, and Jennifer caught herself looking at her own reflection more than once, her mind still making the transition from the muddy, crowded refugee camp to the pristine, quiet halls of the royal palace.

''I've set aside a room so you can prepare,'' Sophie said, glancing down at an electronic organizer Jennifer hadn't noticed before. ''The dinner is scheduled for the Imperial Ballroom, 8:00 p.m. sharp. I've arranged for a selection of evening gowns to be delivered to the room at five. A stylist will be at your disposal at six o'clock, and I have the makeup artist booked for six forty-five—''

Jennifer stopped walking.

''Is there a problem?''

Yes, there's a problem. I'm out of my league here.

''No, of course not,'' she couldn't believe the prince had gone to so much trouble. She hated making others go out of their way for her. Her parents raised her to live economically so what extras they had could go to those in need, not so she could kick back and be indulged.

Struggling to find the right words, Jennifer added, ''But I don't need a makeup artist or a beautician or anything like that.'' Heck, just borrowing a dress for the occasion left her guilt-ridden.

Sophie frowned. "You prefer to do your own hair and makeup for the event?"

"Well, it's just that, you see…"

Sophie's smile reassured her. "I do. The prince told me how hard you work, how much you do without day-to-day. He wants you to relax and allow yourself to feel pampered. Besides, I'm quite certain you'll have enough on your mind as it comes time to deliver your speech."

Sophie pushed open another heavy wooden door, then took Jennifer down an oak-paneled hallway. The rooms off this hallway appeared smaller and more intimate than those off the large marble one. Oil paintings of past San Riminian kings and their families adorned the walls, but these depicted informal settings, unlike the rigid, posed portraits she'd seen elsewhere in the palace. The formal vases and elaborate tapestries of the larger hallways gave way to cabinets filled with clay pottery, most of it painted with zebra, giraffe and elephant motifs. Subtly displayed alongside the pottery were carved wooden animals, apparently gifts from royal trips abroad.

"Prince Antony has an affinity for all things African," Sophie offered, apparently noticing Jennifer's interest as she peeked into the glass cabinets and studied their contents. "He receives hundreds of gifts from around the world every year, but these are the items he chooses to display."

Jennifer stopped to study a handwoven basket. What she didn't know about Prince Antony could fill a library of books. She'd never have guessed he'd appreciate anything so…so *earthy*. "I assume most of these were from foreign dignitaries?"

"On the contrary. Most of these were received

from women and children when he toured AIDS centers and orphanages across sub-Saharan Africa.''

Jennifer blinked back her surprise. ''Interesting.'' Perhaps Prince Antony really did mean it when he said he cared what happened to the refugees in the Haffali camp. He'd obviously made several trips to the world's poorest regions.

Sophie pointed to a photograph of the prince and a small child, mounted behind a delicate string of wooden beads. ''This was taken when his highness visited Zimbabwe. The young man shown handing the beads to the prince lost both his parents to AIDS. *Time* magazine was doing a story on the epidemic and ran this on the cover. The picture was good publicity for the royal family. The diTaloras want the public to know that they take their charitable duties very seriously.''

Jennifer's enthusiasm over the prince's charity work faded. Once again, she'd jumped to her own conclusion about his motives. The royal family—and Prince Antony in particular—fixated far more on the effect their charity work had on their own affairs, rather than its effect on those in need. They viewed charity work as nothing more than a duty. Sophie hadn't even mentioned what the *Time* magazine cover did for AIDS awareness.

Well, so be it, she told herself. The prince's help meant the plight of Rasovo's refugees would be brought to the attention of thousands of people. The prince's motive for helping shouldn't matter to her an iota.

And neither should his looks. Or his charm. Or his touch.

She shook the thought of his electrifying touch

from her mind, instead forcing herself to focus on the remaining displays Sophie pointed out as they walked. Safer to think about the carved monkeys filling the display cabinets than the lion of a man who owned them.

Soon, Sophie rounded a corner, opening a set of double doors to reveal a luxurious bedroom. Thick beige damask fabric covered the walls, and a similar fabric appeared on the bedding. A giant canopy topped the bed, rising up to such a height Jennifer wondered how anyone could possibly keep it dust-free. A pair of chestnut-colored leather chairs flanked a two-story floor-to-ceiling window which overlooked the royal gardens. And, as Jennifer had come to expect in the palace, a heavy chandelier illuminated the entire room.

"This will be your room," Sophie said as Jennifer forced herself not to gawk at the rich trappings. "I assumed, given that the dinner won't end until at least midnight, you planned to stay the night."

"I hadn't thought that far ahead," Jennifer admitted. "I suppose I'd only considered this evening." Besides, what normal American girl in her right mind expected to sleep in a royal palace? Let alone as the guest of a sexy crown prince?

"You'll find a bathroom through there," Sophie pointed to a door handle cleverly hidden along the fabric-covered wall, then turned and indicated a similarly disguised door nearby, "and a dressing room through here. You'll find all the usual toiletries, as well as a selection of nightgowns, at your disposal." The efficient secretary strode to the far end of the room, then opened another set of double doors. "I've arranged for the stylist and makeup artist to meet you here.''

Sophie waved a hand to welcome Jennifer into the room, which contained a sumptuous brown velvet sofa. Next to the sofa, an inlaid table was set with a crystal water pitcher, matching glasses and a bowl of fresh fruit. On her left, a generous carved mantel surrounded a centuries-old fireplace.

Jennifer's gaze swooped over the furnishings, then lingered on the large oil painting hanging over the mantel. It depicted a teenage Prince Antony, dressed in his formal robes. Jennifer couldn't help but marvel at how confident, poised and downright good-looking the prince had been, even as an adolescent. She could almost picture him sweeping the robe behind him, mounting a horse, and carrying her off to a very royal, very private hideaway.

Not that she had any desire to be carried off by *any* prince, let alone the duty-bound, media-hungry Prince Antony. She'd much rather command her own destiny.

Turning away from the mantel, she noticed an intricately painted armoire dominated the far wall. A matching vanity with a beautiful gilded mirror was positioned next to the floor-to-ceiling window to catch the natural light of the outdoors.

The feminine room seemed fit for a queen, and Jennifer wondered if the late Queen Aletta, the prince's mother, had ever stayed here. Or if it was frequented by the prince's girlfriends. She could just picture Daniela Heit sprawled across the sofa in one of the thin designer gowns she modeled on the catwalks of Paris and Milan.

Jennifer pushed the thought from her mind, angry

with herself for even caring. What did it matter to her if the prince entertained women here?

"You have thirty minutes before the dresses arrive, so please make yourself comfortable," Sophie noted as she adjusted the curtains, allowing Jennifer a more expansive view of the gardens. "I'll be back just before dinner to show you the way to the Imperial Ballroom."

Sophie turned and strode back through the bedroom, pausing just before the door to the outside hallway.

"Oh, Ms. Allen——" Sophie began.

"Please, call me Jennifer."

"Jennifer, then," Sophie continued, her features suddenly warmer, "if you need anything at all—something to eat, fresh towels, extra bedding—ring this." She pointed to a velvet cord suspended from the ceiling near the door. "Carlo, Prince Antony's private butler, will be happy to help you."

Jennifer could hardly keep her jaw from dropping right to the silk-carpeted floor.

"Prince Antony's private butler?"

"The prince has instructed the staff to treat you as a VIP. As such, he arranged for you to stay here, in his private wing of the palace, rather than in the palace's guest quarters. Carlo is in charge of this area."

Sophie started to pull the door closed behind her, then paused and leaned back inside. She looked Jennifer up and down, then whispered, "If anyone asks, I never said it. But if you're as convincing tonight as you must have been at the refugee camp, you could change your life. Prince Antony's, as well."

The secretary ducked out before Jennifer could ask what she meant.

* * *

"Wow," Antony whispered to himself, pulling the edge of the green velvet curtain back for a better look. "She chose the blue."

Jennifer stood at the bottom of the double staircase, waiting her turn as guests were announced before entering the Imperial Ballroom. Despite standing high above her on an interior balcony overlooking the staircase, Antony picked her out of the milling crowd immediately. No man with a drop of testosterone in his body could miss the magnificent redhead in the sparkling sapphire-blue gown. The images he'd had of her sashaying around the palace in a ballgown when he'd first met her had been way off.

Even in his daydreams she hadn't looked this good. And he'd had some wild daydreams about her lately.

He checked his watch, wishing the minutes would tick by faster. He usually liked making a royal entrance, always the last man other than his father to enter the ballroom.

But not tonight.

Tonight, he needed to see Jennifer up close. Needed to learn more about her, what she thought, what she believed in. Needed to listen to her melodic voice, feel the small of her back as they danced, smell her gorgeous red curls and dream of what life could have been.

Tonight might be his last chance to enjoy the company of a real woman, the kind of woman he dreamed he could marry, before he settled down with one of the boring, aristocratic women considered more suitable for someone of his noble birth.

And he didn't want to waste a single moment getting started.

He'd even tapped his resources that afternoon to learn about her background. He'd been stunned to learn that her parents had been relief workers as well—first in Vietnam, then in Cambodia, helping displaced orphans find their parents or, if the parents couldn't be located, finding them new homes in America. Finally, they'd landed in Romania, helping to bring western medical care to the thousands of orphans left behind as communism came to an end.

After pondering the information most of the afternoon, he'd come to realize that Jennifer must have been raised much as he had—to believe that those who had been given advantages in life had a duty to help those without. And that duty had to come before all else. Unfortunately, he'd wanted to escape his duties lately, particularly the duty imposed on him by his father. He couldn't help but wonder how Jennifer would handle things if she were in his position.

Without complaining, he suspected.

The thought made him all the more fascinated with her.

"I don't recognize that young lady. She must be new to the court."

Antony dropped the curtain at the sound of the king's voice. So much for escaping his duties. "I wasn't told you were coming tonight, Father."

"I'm not," King Eduardo replied. "I'm not feeling my best, and I'm afraid it would be obvious to those who know me well. But I heard you invited Lady Bianca, so I wanted to see if she'd arrived. However," the king pulled back the edge of the heavy velvet curtain to take another look at the guests waiting to be announced, "that young lady looks promising. Very tall. Attractive, too. Is that Countess

NICOLE BURNHAM   67

Benedetta's daughter, Francesca? I heard she's been living in France, studying art history at the Sorbonne.''

Antony took a deep breath, forcing himself not to bristle at his father's attempts to find the next diTalora queen. "No. That is Ms. Jennifer Allen, of the United States. She's the director of the Haffali refugee camp, and will be speaking at tonight's dinner.''

"I see,'' the king commented. "Too bad she's untitled. And an American. When I saw her I'd rather hoped... well, no matter. Many of the kingdom's most well-respected, aristocratic women will be in attendance tonight, including Lady Bianca. I do hope you'll make the most of the opportunity?''

"Yes, Father,'' Antony promised, forcing himself not to glance back at Jennifer. "I plan to.''

Chapter Four

Jennifer wandered through the crowd, unsure what to do with herself. Around her, women in evening gowns and jewelry suitable for the Academy Awards flirted with men in tuxedos. Champagne flowed freely, the sound of a string quartet filled the air, and discussion seemed fixed on subjects she couldn't discuss for even a minute.

One group of women bragged to each other about their interior decorators, another tossed around gossip about the upcoming San Riminian debutante ball. Men bantered about the soaring European stock market, their latest acquisitions, and the odds on various teams in the national polo tournament. Everyone in attendance at the benefit dinner seemed to know each other. And no one knew her.

Summoning up her courage, Jennifer approached a tall woman in a well-fitted red gown who looked to be about her own age. The pale, ebony-haired woman had just entered the room, and took a glass of champagne from the tray of a passing waiter. Jennifer did the same.

The woman finally noticed her and smiled. "What a beautiful gown you're wearing. Escada, isn't it?" Offering her hand, she added, "I don't believe we've met. I'm Lady Bianca Caratelli. And a fan of all things Escada."

The prince's rumored girlfriend? It was no wonder. She stood almost as tall as Jennifer, but had the thin, just-ask-me-how-rich-I-am look of a woman who spent hours at the gym every day and ate nothing more substantial than salad.

Jennifer knew she'd never have a body like that, even if she was wealthy enough to have a personal trainer, let alone access to a gym or the time to work out. Her only exercise came from working around the camp.

She shook the young woman's hand, noticing how fragile it felt in her own. "I'm pleased to meet you, Lady Bianca. My name is Jennifer. Jennifer Allen."

"Well. Ms. Allen, you'll have to tell me who designed your gown. If it's not Escada, I may have to declare a new favorite."

Jennifer felt her cheeks warm. She hadn't thought to look at the label of her dress. She'd simply selected one from the rack and put it on. "Thank you, though I have to admit I have no idea who designed it. I didn't have anything suitable for giving a speech at the royal palace, I'm afraid, so it's on loan. But I'll make sure the owner knows you complimented it."

Lady Bianca looked her over, allowing her gaze to wander over the dress. Jennifer wanted to wilt under the socialite's studious gaze. She got the distinct impression Lady Bianca assessed every woman she met as competition for the prince's hand.

"Ah," Lady Bianca finally replied, a well-practiced smile gracing her features. Apparently, she decided Jennifer—with her naiveté about all things fashionable—wasn't a threat, and it was therefore safe to continue their conversation. "You must be the American girl Antony met on his trip to Rasovo last week. I understand he asked you to come speak about your cause for his new scholarship fund."

"Yes, he did," Jennifer replied, surprised to hear Lady Bianca call the prince by his first name. It sounded odd to her ear, though she supposed the prince's girlfriend was entitled to call him by whatever name she wanted.

"How fortunate for you," Lady Bianca's plastic smile widened. "Antony's such a generous man. He just loves to do what he can to help people less fortunate than ourselves."

People like you, Jennifer could almost hear in the woman's voice.

Lady Bianca waved at a friend, then continued, "I'm sure this dinner will help raise awareness for your little organization. I wish you the best of luck with your speech."

With that, the dark-haired beauty sashayed off toward a crowd of young men, all of whom seemed to have taken note of her arrival.

"Great," Jennifer muttered under her breath. Her excitement over having the opportunity to speak about the refugees and their plight rushed out of her.

Lady Bianca thought the Rasovo Relief Society was a "little organization" and even though they had to be close to the same age, she was just an "American" *girl,* not a *woman,* and therefore clearly out of the pampered socialite's league. Did the rest of the guests feel the same way? Were they simply here to wine and dine with the prince and enjoy an evening gossiping amongst themselves?

Jennifer balled her fists. She supposed it was a miracle the prince asked her to come speak at all. He probably didn't respect her or her work any more than Lady Bianca did.

Much as she hated to admit it, the thought that Antony didn't care tore at her heart. He'd seemed so excited about what he could do for the Rasovars. And he hadn't given her any indication, from his phone call, at least, that he was only in it for the publicity. He seemed genuinely interested in helping her, and in having her stay in the palace as his guest.

Obviously, given Lady Bianca's demeaning words and what Sophie said about the family's dedication to their charitable duty, she'd misinterpreted his invitation. Sure, she'd dreamed of dining with Antony at a royal soiree. Who wouldn't? The man made her insides turn to butter.

But apparently, Prince Antony preferred to dine with women like Lady Bianca, but have women—or *girls*—like Jennifer make him look like a hero for dutifully supporting their "little organizations."

"Fine," she muttered to herself. "Then I'll make him a hero." After tonight, she could go home, forget the prince, and just cross her fingers she spoke eloquently enough to raise awareness about the refugee camp. Then she'd get the volunteers she so desperately needed, and to heck with the prince.

"Make who a hero?"

The sound of Antony's regal voice, thick with his

seductive San Riminian accent, made her jump nearly out of her skin. How long had he been standing behind her? How much more had she said aloud, not even realizing he could hear every word?

"I'm sorry, I didn't mean to startle you," he grinned and took her elbow with one of his large, warm hands.

"I—I didn't see you there," Jennifer fumbled for words as his touch blew her concentration to smithereens. How could she have missed the sudden quiet in the room? Had she been so buried in her own thoughts she missed the announcement of the prince's arrival?

"You looked like your mind was a million miles away, Ms. Allen. Pondering your upcoming speech, I take it?"

"Of course." Well, she *was* thinking about her speech. Sort of. And how she could make herself focus on it, instead of on him. "But please, call me Jennifer," she added, hoping to change the subject. "No one calls me Ms. Allen."

"Fine. I will call you Jennifer, then." Her name came out sounding more like *"Zhennifer,"* given his accent, but his warm smile more than made up for his pronunciation.

She could live with being called *"Zhennifer."*

"You'll have to tell me about the hero-making business another time, however," Antony gestured over her left shoulder. "I'd like you to meet my brother, Prince Federico, and his wife, Princess Lucrezia."

Jennifer turned, surprised to see the royal couple standing just behind her. She introduced herself, then added, "I'm honored. I didn't realize you were going to be in attendance."

Princess Lucrezia, a Lady Bianca clone if Jennifer had ever seen one, apparently hadn't planned on being in attendance either, judging from the bored look on her face.

Prince Federico, however, seemed excited. "On the contrary, Ms. Allen," Antony's younger brother welcomed her, "we're glad you could make the trip to speak about the Rasovo Relief Society. It's nice to know we can do something to help the refugees. After all, they are our neighbors."

"I'm afraid our sister, Princess Isabella, and our younger brother, Prince Stefano, couldn't be here tonight, though you should know they were invited," Antony explained. "Isabella's speaking at an art museum fundraiser in New York, and Stefano—"

"Stefano is off being Stefano who knows where," Federico interrupted with a disapproving shake of his head. "Fortunately father doesn't know, or Stefano would get quite a lecture for his unexcused absence."

Antony grinned. "Father will find out, just as he always does. And we'll cover for Stefano, just as we always do."

With that, he and Federico began to reminisce about pranks Prince Stefano pulled when he was a young boy. From the sound of it, Antony, Federico and Isabella bailed Stefano out of trouble on numerous occasions, including one time when Stefano tried to substitute his Play-Doh for the pâté de foie gras at a state dinner.

Jennifer laughed, amazed to see the love shared by the royal siblings. The diTalora clan's banter sounded like that of a typical family, complete with the rebellious younger brother, the do-gooder only daughter, the domineering father and the protective older brothers. That is, if being heirs to a thousand-year-old throne and living in a palace with servants catering to your every whim constituted typical.

For a brief moment, Jennifer wondered what it would be like to be part of the diTalora family. Princess Lucrezia seemed weary of it, but Jennifer thought it would be fantastic to be part of a family as wonderful and loving as her own had been. Plus, as a member of the royal family, she'd have the resources to help those in need, like the Rasovars.

And then there was the fantasy of actually being married to Prince Antony. What would it be like to wake up next to him each morning? To run her hands through his thick, dark hair and pull him close against her? To lose herself in his blue-eyed gaze? To have him stand by her side as she continued to pursue her own dreams? And, most of all, to have him read to their own children with as much love and caring as he had to Josef?

While the men continued to discuss Stefano's exploits, Princess Lucrezia turned toward her, obviously uncomfortable at being left out of the conversation. "Tell me, Ms. Allen," she began, "are you enjoying your visit to San Rimini?"

She reluctantly yanked her thoughts away from Antony. "Of course. I've been to San Rimini a couple of times before, but never inside the royal palace. It's amazing."

"Yes, a big difference from living in a refugee camp, I understand." The princess's tone bordered on condescending.

"A huge difference. We're happy to have flashlights, let alone chandeliers,'' she joked, hoping the princess would lighten up.

Princess Lucrezia didn't crack a smile. "I see. Will you be able to stay long? Or are you needed back at your camp?"

"I'll stay tonight, obviously," Jennifer replied, pretending not to be offended by the princess's obvious insinuation that she shouldn't spend too long at the palace. "But I'll head back first thing in the morning. As you know, we've very short-staffed."

Princess Lucrezia raised her eyebrows. "I cannot imagine many people would want to work in such terrible conditions. It's practically punishment to require scholarship recipients to work in such a place, you know."

Jennifer must have looked as dumbfounded as she felt at hearing such a statement, because the princess quickly added, "It is a good plan, however. The more workers you have, the easier it gets, yes? So it is not really punishment."

"Well, I hope no one views it as punishment at all," Jennifer managed to respond, keeping her tone polite despite the princess's ignorant statements. "The students will be giving something of themselves to the international community, and the international community will be giving something valuable to the students in return—a first-class education here in San Rimini."

Before Princess Lucrezia could reply, a bell sounded in the ballroom. "It's time for us to take our seats," Antony said, returning to her side. "This way."

He cupped Jennifer's elbow in his hand once again, almost possessively. The simple gesture sent a shock-wave of heat and nervous energy coursing through her body. She marveled at his ability to welcome her into his world, make her appear to belong in this elite crowd, even as the other guests—including Antony's own sister-in-law—seemed to push her away.

"You'll be sitting on the dais, with me," Antony leaned in close, whispering in her ear in the same intimate way he'd done on the helipad in Rasovo. "I'll introduce you, at which time you should stand and come to the podium. Then—what is it you Americans say?—knock over dead?"

"Something like that," Jennifer managed, though her nerves sizzled every time he spoke to her with his enticing San Riminian accent. How could she possibly focus on her speech with the prince whispering in her ear to knock 'em dead?

Reaching down to her purse, she felt inside for her notes. Maybe a quick run-through of the points she wanted to address would settle her nerves and distract her from Antony's charms.

She stopped short. Her fingers ran over a lipstick, a brush, a small mirror...but no notecards. Had she left them in the room? She opened the purse wide to take a better look, then ran her hand around the inside once more.

No notecards.

"What is it?" Antony's forehead crinkled in concern.

She glanced around the room, noticing that nearly everyone had taken their seats. They were staring at her, likely wondering about the identity of the batty redhead keeping the prince from the podium. She worried the inside of her lip for a moment. No time to return to the room now. She'd have to wing it.

"Nothing," she lied, hoping the prince couldn't see her mounting panic. Forcing a smile to her face, she added, "Time to knock over dead."

"Beautiful," Antony mumbled an answer to Lady Bianca's question without really knowing what she'd asked. Something about Countess DuVaye's trendy new hairstyle.

Antony sipped his wine slowly, trying to focus on Bianca's nonstop droning. What had he been thinking when he asked Sophie to seat her on the dais next to him?

True, it would make his father, and the parliament members present at the dinner, believe that he had a romantic interest in her and allay their fears that he'd never produce an heir. And true, he probably *would* end up marrying Bianca or Countess DuVaye or one of their friends by year-end. If he must.

But he'd underestimated the forcefulness of his attraction to Jennifer. Seating her on his left side for dinner made it nearly impossible to pay attention to Bianca on his right.

Though he'd found Jennifer somewhat brash when he visited her camp, in this setting, he could now see that she represented everything a proper diTalora queen should be, and everything he personally looked for in a bride. She was elegant, attractive, intelligent, and best of all, her heart seemed to be made of gold.

He envied her energy and convictions. True, he cared about his charitable causes, just as she did. But, even if he was able to as a royal, he wasn't sure he could ever bring himself to do what she did—toiling in dangerous parts of the world, spending long hours working with her hands—to ensure that people in need were clothed and fed. She could have been anything she wanted in life, with her talents, intelligence and breathtaking beauty. He doubted any other woman in the room would choose to follow the path she had, and it made them pale in comparison to her.

He let out a deep breath. Just thinking about Jennifer made his arms ache with a need to hold her, caress her, kiss her. He'd dreamed of a woman like her all his life, a woman who'd challenge and satisfy him in every way, intellectually, spiritually and physically.

She just didn't have the proper bloodline.

And that made marriage to her—a fantasy he'd admittedly indulged in a few times since his father's pronouncement—nothing more than that. Pure fantasy.

He hazarded a glance to his right, where Jennifer sat quietly eating her salad. Her red hair shone under the bright lights topping the dais, the loose tendrils highlighted so as to make her appear almost angelic.

Pure fantasy.

"Antony, dear," Bianca nudged his arm, forcing his attention back to her. "Are you all right? I don't believe you've heard one word I've said all evening."

Antony offered her a half-hearted smile. "Just nerves, I suppose. As you know, this is an important night for my new scholarship fund."

Bianca leaned in closer than he liked and whispered, "It's her, isn't it? Are you worried she'll deliver a poor speech? I doubt she's ever spoken to such a large and esteemed audience as this one."

"That's not it," he shot back, keeping his voice low so Jennifer wouldn't overhear.

"Well, if your problem *is* simple nerves," Bianca's

voice indicated she suspected it wasn't, "then a long, slow dance with me is the perfect cure."

Bianca ran her hand along his arm, and Antony noticed a press photographer in the corner of the room lining up a shot.

He forced himself not to grimace. *You set yourself up for this,* he reminded himself. Getting caught in a more-than-just-friends pose with Lady Bianca would definitely put his father's mind at ease. It might even buy him some wiggle room in that ridiculous ultimatum, if it convinced his father he was at least trying to find a proper bride.

But somehow, seeing the photographer snap away in the corner made his affiliation with Bianca official. Every paper and news program in Europe would flash a picture of them huddled together in apparent deep conversation tomorrow. The thought turned his gut to stone and made his blood run cold.

He shifted in his chair, making it difficult for Bianca to keep her hand on his arm.

"Then the first dance after dinner is yours," he promised, though suddenly the overpoofed, posturing Lady Bianca Caratelli was the last woman he wanted.

He wanted Jennifer.

He wanted her even more than he had while watching her from behind the balcony curtain. And he wanted her for more than just tonight.

Unable to tolerate Bianca any longer, he whispered, "I need to introduce Ms. Allen."

"I'll be right here," she breathed back.

That's what he was afraid of.

Chapter Five

Antony stood, and a few dinner guests clanked on their champagne flutes to quiet the room. Antony looked down at Jennifer, seated between him and the podium. Her hands were clasped tightly in her lap, the knuckles white.

"Are you ready to rocking roll?" he asked in his best English.

Jennifer's mouth quirked with merriment, causing his stomach to constrict with renewed desire. "I think you need a few more lessons in English euphemisms, Your Highness."

"I agree, my English could be better. I do not know the word *'you-fem-ism,'*" he pronounced it slowly, hoping he didn't sound like a fool. "What does it mean?"

Her grin widened, causing her eyes to crinkle at the corners. Somehow, he couldn't picture Bianca or any of her friends wearing such a genuine smile. Even if something he said made them want to laugh, they'd be too afraid of the wrinkles a real smile might cause.

"Just introduce me already, Your Highness," Jennifer whispered.

Looking up, he realized that the room had grown completely quiet. Everyone stared at him, waiting to hear what he had to say.

Everyone except Lady Bianca. She glared.

He approached the microphone, then began speaking about the Rasovo Relief Society. He'd only planned to give Jennifer a simple introduction, but as he began telling the audience about his trip to Rasovo, the words came pouring out. He desperately wanted his future subjects to understand the humanity of the Rasovar refugees, the optimism of children like Josef, and the kindness of the staff who helped them.

But most of all, he wanted the elite crowd to know it didn't have to be that way. Their eagerness to support his scholarship fund, and therefore organizations like the Rasovo Relief Society, could make all the difference. Not only would they be furthering the education of San Rimini's best and brightest students, they'd be directly providing their Rasovar neighbors with the assistance they needed to survive.

And they'd be making Jennifer's work so much more worthwhile.

"Look to your right and your left," he instructed the audience. "The people you see are your neighbors. They've offered you their support during hard times, and they've celebrated with you during the good. You would do the same for them, I assume?"

Murmurs of agreement filled the room.

"As a representative of the San Riminian government and as your crown prince, I look to my right and see Slovenia as my neighbor. I look to my left, and I see Italy. Of course, I also see Rasovo, a small but beautiful country with a history as rich as our own.''

He scanned the faces in the crowd, hoping to drive his message home. ''As any good neighbor would, the Rasovars have supported us during our nation's toughest times and celebrated with us during our successes. They sent us foodstuffs during the Great Famine in the time of Queen Danae, and I hope for them to celebrate with us next year, as we mark the thousandth year of San Riminian independence. Unfortunately, that can only happen if we treat the Rasovars as good neighbors, showing them the kindness and respect they have accorded us over these thousand years.''

He cleared his throat, then looked at Jennifer. Her soft blue eyes met his, and he found himself filled with a desire and an enthusiasm for Jennifer and her cause that ran deeper than anything he'd experienced as a crown prince, or as a man.

A desire that was also completely improper.

He forced his gaze away from Jennifer's and looked back to the audience, who seemed fixed on his every word. ''Ms. Jennifer Allen, an American, has gone above and beyond the call of duty in this regard, treating the Rasovars as if they were her own neighbors, rather than ours.''

He wanted to say so much more about her, but it was Jennifer's night, and he had to let her speak. ''The scholarship recipients who go to work for the Rasovo Relief Society will assuredly learn from her example, as we all should. I give you Ms. Jennifer Allen.''

She stood, her blue eyes wide with surprise. She obviously hadn't expected him to take so long introducing her.

"Good job, Your Highness," she whispered as she approached the microphone.

Straining to be heard over the applause, he leaned in close to her ear, "I apologize. I spoke too long."

Her eyes crinkled into the smile he was beginning to love. However, this time they glistened. He wasn't sure if he saw tears there, or merely the reflection of the bright lights over the dais. "Not at all. You spoke from the heart."

He took his seat, then watched as she took the microphone.

"I appreciate your willingness to hear me speak in English instead of Italian," she began, "though I'm not sure how much is left to say. You are quite lucky to have Prince Antony as your future leader. His creative mind has formulated a plan that will help both the Rasovars and the San Riminians, and I for one am grateful."

Antony sat back in his chair, amazed Jennifer actually liked what he had to say, despite the fact he'd hogged the spotlight.

When he'd first returned to the royal palace, he'd been determined to show her what he could do, prove to her he wasn't just a figurehead or a check-writing machine. But now, now that his dreams for the scholarship fund were coming to fruition, he felt so much more. More than he had for any charitable cause in his life.

Jennifer had taught him to care. He smiled to himself with the realization.

"My goodness, Antony," Lady Bianca murmured

in his ear, just as her hand snaked its way back to his arm. "I don't believe I've ever heard you speak like that."

He turned to Bianca, happy she could see the change he felt on the inside. "No, I don't believe I ever have."

Bianca frowned but said nothing. Instead, she looked past him to Jennifer, apparently intent on hearing about the scholarship fund and how it could help the refugees.

Antony turned his attention back to the podium as well. Jennifer spoke with a deep-seated belief that mesmerized her audience. Women were transfixed by the stories of the refugees. Men stared, partially awed by Jennifer's words and, Antony was certain, partially by her beauty.

He let his gaze wander over her figure again. From his seat he had the perfect vantage point to study her narrow waist and lean, athletic hips, emphasized to perfection by the exquisite sapphire gown. He studied her leg, just visible through a slit in the side of the long dress. What would it be like to awaken each morning able to see those legs?

Then he noticed her foot, tapping a nervous beat against the floor. He looked up to her face, but didn't see an ounce of trepidation, nothing that would let the audience see her apparent case of stage fright.

"She's terribly nervous," Bianca whispered over his shoulder, apparently noticing Jennifer's tapping foot just as he did. "It's a good thing you did most of the talking. She's out of her element."

Antony turned to correct her, and hopefully to quiet her, but as Bianca ran her hand along his arm once more and flashed him an intimate smile, he thought better of it. He couldn't risk alienating her in public, no matter how badly he wanted to be free of her—and hidden away with Jennifer—tonight.

Jennifer, he reminded himself, for all the positive things she'd taught him about charity, would only be around temporarily. Then she'd return to her life in Rasovo, working with refugees. He'd be here, in the midst of San Rimini's elite. And he'd be expected to marry one of them soon if he couldn't convince his father there was no need for an ultimatum.

"You know," Bianca continued, "as soon as she's finished, we'll get our dance."

Antony swallowed hard. "How could I possibly forget?"

The grin plastered across Jennifer's face as she shook the parliament member's hand probably pegged her as being less-than-aristocratic, but she didn't care.

Despite forgetting her notes, despite Antony practically robbing her of the speech she'd improvised with his long introduction, the talk had gone off without a hitch. And dozens of San Rimini's well-to-do pulled out their checkbooks in response.

"Just tell me where to send my money," the rotund man told Jennifer while he pumped her hand. "I'm honored to contribute to such a worthy cause, as many of my peers will be, I'm certain."

"Wonderful, wonderful speech," the man's equally plump wife gushed. "We come to these palace charity events all the time, dear, but never have we heard anyone speak so eloquently. And the prince!" The woman glanced across the room, where Antony was surrounded by hangers-on, then fanned herself. "My goodness, but I've never heard him sound as sincere as he did tonight. I think our crown prince is a changed man!''

"He certainly is," the parliament member agreed, then turned to speak with another member of the crowd around Jennifer.

Jennifer thanked the man's wife for their kindness, but wondered if Antony really had changed. She wanted to believe the woman's words, badly. Wanted to know that he wasn't simply fixated on the media and his public image, as the tabloids had accused in the past. Wanted to know that he didn't simply view charity work as a duty, as something he'd been trained to do. Rather, she wanted charity to be something his heart yearned to do, as hers did.

As she shook hands with another well-wisher, an older gentleman known to be a close friend of the king's, she overheard a deep male voice behind her comment about Antony's apparent about-face. Her heart soared. If he'd convinced this crowd, a crowd he'd run with since youth, that he was a changed man, perhaps he was.

After the older gentleman took his leave, Jennifer spun around to see who'd made the comment about Antony. She stopped short, finding herself face-to-face with Prince Federico.

"Ms. Allen," Federico took her hand and kissed it. "Your speech was a success. Congratulations."

"Thank you," she blinked, hardly believing that a San Riminian prince had kissed her hand, even if it wasn't Antony. "I hope you don't mind, but I overheard you a moment ago. You said that Antony has changed. What did you mean?"

"As you know, my brother has always done charitable work," Federico replied, "but I've never seen him quite so taken with it. I believe, if he could, he would volunteer to work at your camp himself.''

Jennifer tried to picture Antony working in the camp. Even though he had arrived for his tour dressed in a far more casual outfit than the tailored tuxedo and royal sash he sported tonight, she couldn't envision him digging latrines or helping to carry an injured, frightened refugee the last mile into Haffali.

Changed? Maybe. But willing to volunteer in her camp? Willing to get his hands dirty and truly give of himself? He'd never change *that* much.

As the band began to play, Federico looked past her, scouring the room.

"I don't see my wife," Federico commented. "She may be in the powder room. However, as a member of the royal family, I always like to lead my guests to the dance floor. Would you be so kind as to accompany me?''

A dance with Antony's younger brother? Why not? "I'd love to.''

Jennifer took the prince's extended arm, then let him lead her onto the floor. Across the ballroom, she caught sight of Antony, his dark hair reflecting the now-lowered lights of the Imperial Ballroom as he made his way through the crowd toward the dance floor.

Once again, she found herself filled with longing as she watched his smooth, confident walk. She'd never believed a man could be both elegant and physically powerful at the same time. Antony pulled it off with panache.

Her mind raced as Federico spun her onto the floor for the first dance of the evening, keeping a polite distance between them. He was a consummate dancer.

Still, Jennifer couldn't help but wonder what it would be like to have Antony as her partner. Would his dance steps be as graceful as his walk? She felt certain they would, but doubted she'd ever get the chance to find out.

On the other hand, since she was the keynote speaker, he might feel obliged to dance with her. Her heart leapt at the thought, though she'd fought for days to control her response to Antony. Princes didn't exactly date social workers. Especially not American social workers from a family barely able to scrape two pennies together.

Even more importantly, she knew indulging in daydreams about Antony were a sure way to blow her concentration while she networked with the wealthy San Riminians. She'd nearly blown the evening anyway, spending so much time focusing on Antony she'd left her notes behind in the room. But now that the speech was in the can...

She glanced past Federico to study Antony again. He'd almost reached the dance floor, and Jennifer couldn't help but wish he'd cut in on her dance with Federico. Then his gaze locked onto her, and he swallowed hard enough she could see it.

She wanted to tear her gaze away from his, but couldn't. Something about seeing him under the soft light of the chandeliers, unaffected by the stares of admirers all around him, brought out the sexuality she knew had to bubble under his well-schooled surface.

Then Lady Bianca appeared.

So much for her wish to dance with Antony. Lady Bianca's lean frame had been obscured by the group gathered around Antony, but now Jennifer saw the dark-haired beauty emerge from the crowd, her small hand resting firmly but comfortably on Prince Antony's arm. Even worse, Lady Bianca made a point of staring down the other women she passed on the way to the dance floor, as if to say *he's mine.*

Jennifer grimaced and looked away. If wishes were horses...

"What does this mean, wishes are horses?" Federico asked.

Had she said it out loud?

"If you wish Lady Bianca to become a horse, I must disagree," he added, his San Riminian accent heavy, but his grin easy to understand.

Federico must have caught her watching Antony and Lady Bianca. Now he was teasing her! Her face flushed hot.

"That's not what I meant."

"I believe she would be better as a weasel," he continued, twirling her so he could better see Antony and Lady Bianca. "Yes, definitely a weasel. However, that is not an official comment from the palace. I will deny it if asked."

Jennifer stifled a laugh. "You're terrible! I didn't think a prince would ever say such things. Particularly about someone who might become his sister-in-law someday."

"Royals cannot speak this way, which is why I will deny it. However," his voice dropped a notch, "you are wrong about Lady Bianca. I doubt Antony will marry her, though she desires it."

"Why? She's beautiful, poised, from a good family...everything a prince would want, I'd imagine."

"Yes," he nodded. "She is much like Lucrezia. Appropriate for me, but not for Antony. For Antony, a woman must..." Federico frowned, as if searching for the correct words, "she must make his heart... make it go to a different place."

"Move him?"

"Yes, move him."

As they continued to dance, Jennifer got another good look at Prince Antony and Lady Bianca. Everything about Lady Bianca oozed perfection—perfect hair, perfect smile, perfect bloodline, even perfect friends. Worst of all, the socialite seemed a perfect fit for Antony, though it pained Jennifer to think so.

"If a woman like Lady Bianca doesn't move him, no one will," Jennifer commented.

"I believe another woman already has."

"Oh."

Jennifer's throat constricted, even as Federico continued to whirl her about the room as if they hadn't a care in the world. So much for her romantic dreams of Antony. Not that they were realistic in the first place, she reminded herself, but still, it was nice to have the dream. Hearing Federico and the others say Antony had changed, that he cared about her cause and truly wanted to help out, made her dream seem all the more powerful. And now that he apparently loved another woman, all the harder to forget.

"Antony, Bianca," Federico called over her shoulder, surprising her.

Jennifer turned her head to discover that Federico had expertly spun them across the ballroom floor to dance beside Antony and Lady Bianca.

"Good evening, Prince Federico," Lady Bianca nodded politely, though it was obvious from her expression she didn't appreciate the interruption. "And Ms. Allen. Congratulations on a wonderful speech. You and Antony did splendidly." She pulled Antony a little closer, then looked up at him and winked, making it crystal clear which of the two she really believed had done splendidly.

"It's nice of you to say so," Jennifer replied, though every fiber in her body wanted to slug the woman. All through the speech, she'd heard someone nearby whispering. Then when she'd glanced at Lady Bianca to see if she was the source, she could have sworn the woman was mid-eyeroll.

"Bianca, I don't believe we've had a chance to talk tonight. You don't mind if I cut in, do you, Antony?" Federico let go of Jennifer and reached for Bianca, even as he asked his brother's permission.

"Of course, go ahead."

Antony thanked Lady Bianca for the dance, then stepped away. Just for a moment, Jennifer thought a look of relief washed over his face. But just as soon as it registered with her, it was gone.

She had to have imagined it. Just as she had to have imagined that Antony had stared at her as she danced with Federico. He'd probably been looking right past her at some drop-dead gorgeous duchess in the crowd. After all, if Federico's hunch was right, Antony loved another woman.

"We both appear to be without our partners," Antony commented, turning to her and holding out his arm. "Would you do me the honor?"

He didn't want to grab some bejeweled goddess from the crowd? "Um, sure. If you're sure, that is. I think Prince Federico abandoned me because I almost stepped on his feet."

"That is because Federico is not as accomplished a dancer as I am." His arm went around her waist, and his hand moved to rest against her lower back.

Then, taking her hand in his free one, he added, "I promise, you will not step on my feet."

Jennifer said nothing, instead placing her other hand on Antony's firm, broad shoulder and allowing him to twirl her about the floor. The grand waltz music that filled the great hall, combined with the warm touch of Antony's hand against her lower back, made her want to close her eyes and let herself be swept away for the night. Made her want to forget the pain, suffering and hardship she'd be returning to tomorrow, no matter how much the Rasovars meant to her.

"You see? I am far better than Federico."

Jennifer couldn't help but smile at Antony. "Anyone ever tell you you've got a lot of confidence in yourself?"

He frowned. "It is my job as crown prince to be confident. The citizens of San Rimini expect it. Besides, I have always believed Americans to show a great deal more confidence than any European. Except you."

"Me?"

He pulled her a little closer, sending a flash of warmth along her spine. She could almost feel his breath against her cheek as he spoke. "When you took me on the tour of your camp, you had no problem telling me where I should go and what I should see. You were in complete control."

"But?"

"But here, you are quite nervous."

She forced herself to straighten a bit, even as they danced. "What makes you say that?"

"You did not stand still during your speech. The others did not notice it, but I did."

So he'd been watching her. Somehow, dancing

with him so closely now, it didn't surprise her. "I'll let you in on a little secret, Your Highness. Remember how I hesitated as we were walking to the dais before dinner?"

"Yes?"

"I realized I'd left the notes for my speech in my room. I had to ad-lib it."

"Ad-lib?" He shook his head, not quite understanding.

"Ad-lib. Improvise. Make it up as I went."

He blinked. "You did?"

"Yes. Even though your introduction was impossibly long and you said nearly everything I wanted to say."

"I apologize—"

She shook her head at him. "I was teasing. You did wonderfully. We make a good team."

As soon as the words were out of her mouth, she realized what she'd said. *A team.*

Well, they did make a good team professionally, even if they'd never be one personally. Prince Antony had the clout to get things done for the Rasovars; she had the passion. Although, if she judged Antony based solely on tonight's performance and ignored the way he'd apparently viewed charity in the past, he had a passion for it, too.

The music slowed, and Antony moved his hand on her back, slowing their pace to match the music. "You are right, Jennifer," his voice quieted, as if it too was affected by the change in the music. "We make a good team."

Jennifer looked into Antony's eyes, and what she saw there left no doubt as to his meaning.

Chapter Six

Antony wanted to bite his tongue as soon as the words left his mouth. What right did he have telling Jennifer they made a good team? He frantically hoped she'd take his statement as something professional, though his thoughts definitely leaned toward a more intimate meaning.

He spun them to another corner of the dance floor, away from where Lady Bianca continued to dance with Federico. How his brother knew he needed rescuing was beyond him, but he would be grateful to his dying day. It gave him the chance to feel Jennifer in his arms, even though he could never pursue a romantic relationship with her.

Not that she'd be interested in him. His entire life, women had stared at him, flirted with him, pursued him, and above all made it clear to him that they would mold themselves into whatever image he might find most desirous in a bride.

But not Jennifer. Jennifer alone let him see her true

personality. She didn't seem intimidated by him, nor willing to change her views simply to impress him.

He liked the change of pace, spending time around her and listening to her opinions instead of those of the shallow women who typically frequented the court. He only wished it could last.

Gazing down at her, he said, "If I have not yet told you, you look absolutely stunning in that dress."

He'd wanted to engage her in a meatier conversation, pick her brain for ideas to help other groups in need, such as the San Rimini Cancer Council. But somehow, a comment on her dress popped out. What was it about looking at her sweet, upturned face that made him lose all logical thought?

The corners of her mouth curved into a small, tentative smile. "Thank you. When you said you were going to have a selection of gowns available for me, I didn't imagine there'd be so many. Or that they'd be so beautiful."

So he'd gotten carried away. What man wouldn't, given the opportunity to select a gown that would show off a figure like Jennifer's?

"What made you choose that one?" he asked.

"You mean out of the thirty-two dresses that were brought to my room?" She laughed, the lightness of it enticing him even more. The cold palace halls needed laughter like hers to enliven them, make them feel more like a home than a stone-and-marble museum. "I suppose the color. It was the only blue one. And—" she tilted her chin down just enough to study the dress "—it was a simpler cut than the others, and I'm a simple kind of girl." She looked back up at him, her eyes the same vivid shade of blue as the dress. "Why do you ask?"

"It was my favorite."

"You saw the dresses?" She furrowed her forehead. "When?"

"Yesterday. I selected them."

Her eyes widened in surprise. "I assumed you have a staff to do those sorts of things."

"You assumed I take bodyguards everywhere, too."

"Point taken. I suppose I have a lot to learn about you."

Now he couldn't help but grin. "Well, now you know that I like the color blue. And that I like simple, as well."

"Okay. How about a favorite food?"

"Easy. Lasagna."

"Lasagna's not simple," she pointed out.

"Compared to what I'm normally served, it's quite simple."

"Well, someday I hope you find a simple girl who likes blue and bakes a mean lasagna."

He spun her, unwilling to meet her eyes for a moment. He'd already found a simple girl who wore blue, he just couldn't marry her. Couldn't even think about marrying her. And any woman considered proper for him to marry would be far from simple.

Jennifer stepped gracefully back into his arms.

"You have a strange look on your face, Your Highness. Did I say something inappropriate?"

"A mean lasagna?" he managed to recover. "How is a lasagna mean?"

She shook her head, "In America, a 'mean' lasagna is a 'good' lasagna. We use it to describe other things besides food, though. For instance," she nodded

GET FREE BOOKS and a FREE GIFT WHEN YOU PLAY THE...

The Silhouette Reader Service™ — Here's how it works:

Accepting your 2 free books and gift places you under no obligation to buy anything. You may keep the books and gift and return the shipping statement marked "cancel." If you do not cancel, about a month later we'll send you 6 additional novels and bill you just $3.15 each in the U.S., or $3.50 each in Canada, plus 25¢ shipping & handling per book and applicable taxes if any.* That's the complete price and — compared to cover prices of $3.99 each in the U.S. and $4.50 each in Canada — it's quite a bargain! You may cancel at any time, but if you choose to continue, every month we'll send you 6 more books, which you may either purchase at the discount price or return to us and cancel your subscription.

*Terms and prices subject to change without notice. Sales tax applicable in N.Y. Canadian residents will be charged applicable provincial taxes and GST.

If offer card is missing write to: Silhouette Reader Service, 3010 Walden Ave., P.O. Box 1867, Buffalo NY 14240-1867

BUSINESS REPLY MAIL
FIRST-CLASS MAIL   PERMIT NO. 717-003   BUFFALO, NY

POSTAGE WILL BE PAID BY ADDRESSEE

SILHOUETTE READER SERVICE
3010 WALDEN AVE
PO BOX 1867
BUFFALO NY 14240-9952

NO POSTAGE
NECESSARY
IF MAILED
IN THE
UNITED STATES

across the dance floor. "Your brother Federico is a mean dancer."

"I see," he grinned from ear to ear. "You, Jennifer Allen, are just plain mean!"

She started to retort, amazed at his quick grasp of the nuances of English, but the slow, romantic music ended and a crowd-pleasing waltz began, cutting her off.

Other couples flooded the floor. Federico took his leave to speak with a prominent member of parliament—someone on the Succession Committee, Antony noted—leaving Lady Bianca free once more. And headed in his direction.

"I should circulate among my guests," he said as he reluctantly let her go. "Thank you for such lively conversation."

"And thank you for a wonderful evening. The Rasovars will be touched by your generosity."

He ran a hand along her cheek, unable to stop himself. "I just want to help them. And help you."

Forcing his hand away from her soft face, he spun on his heel and made his way toward a disapproving Lady Bianca.

Secluded in the women's restroom, Jennifer leaned her forehead against the inside of the large, ornately-carved door to the bathroom stall, unwilling to let anyone see how flustered the dance with Antony had left her.

She couldn't have imagined the look in his eyes. He'd *wanted* to dance with her! Wanted to hold her like a man held a woman, not like a prince held a visiting guest at a state function, as Federico had during their dance.

She hugged herself, hardly believing it. As her hands ran over the cool fabric of the dress, she remembered that he'd even picked it out himself.

"What a man," she whispered to herself. Antony was far more sensitive than his public image made him appear. Either that, or he'd changed drastically over the last week, as guests had mentioned to her over and over that evening. Heck, even Federico had commented on Antony's change in demeanor.

Her heart constricted in her chest. If he'd changed enough to care about her cause and support it with his whole heart, could he possibly care about her, too? Even though she could never have a real relationship with Prince Antony—she cared far too much about the Rasovars to ever leave the camp—she found she still wanted him to desire her. Heck, she'd even flirted with him!

She let out a deep breath as the image of his firm jaw and powerful shoulders filled her thoughts once more. To dance with him again, to feel his hand guiding her steps across the floor, to experience the quiet power of his lean muscle as she rested her palm against his shoulder, maybe even to kiss him…it was too much to comprehend.

Then she remembered Federico's words. He said that another woman had already moved the prince's heart.

And she knew it wasn't her. If a wealthy and beautiful woman like Lady Bianca couldn't entice him, what hope did she have?

Jennifer straightened. How upside down did the prince turn her emotions that she'd come to this point, leaning her head on the door of a bathroom stall? It had to end. She bent down to fix her panty hose, resolving to return to the ballroom and focus on networking for the Rasovars, rather than on her inexplicable attraction to Antony.

Then she heard a familiar voice coming from the direction of the sinks. The woman spoke in San Riminian-accented Italian, but Jennifer understood enough of the language to follow the conversation.

And the conversation wasn't friendly.

"That American just threw herself at poor Antony," Lady Bianca griped. "I mean, while he visited her camp, she apparently went on and on about how she needed more staff. What could he do but oblige?"

An unfamiliar female voice answered, "I suppose you're right. But he certainly didn't have to *dance* with her. He should have been dancing with you."

"Or you, Ariana. He loves me, of course, but I won't monopolize his time. Still, when he dances with other women, he needs to be selective. There's a difference between dancing with *her*, an American commoner, and someone more appropriate to his position, like you."

"You're absolutely right," the other woman, who had to be Countess Ariana DuVaye, a woman Jennifer remembered to be a friend of Lady Bianca's, agreed. "I've known Antony long enough to know he'd never spend time with that woman if he didn't feel obligated to do so. She must have thrown herself at him, convinced him that he had to support her silly little camp. What nerve!"

Jennifer couldn't stand to hear them any longer. Another word from either woman about how she must've "thrown" herself at Antony and her temper would explode. She'd never thrown herself at a man in her life, for any reason.

Opening the door to the stall, she squared her shoulders, then strode purposefully to the marble sinks to stand between Lady Bianca and her friend.

"Why, hello Jennifer!" Lady Bianca twittered in English. "I was just telling Countess DuVaye what a great influence you've had on Antony."

"Yes," Jennifer kept her eyes focused on the mirror in front of her. "I understand enough Italian to know exactly what you were just telling Countess DuVaye."

"Oh?"

Suddenly feeling empowered, she continued, "And it wasn't very polite. I did not throw myself at Prince Antony or anyone else for that matter. Besides, he's a grown man who is being groomed to rule this country one day. If you think I can coerce him into spending one minute doing something he doesn't wish to do, you underestimate him."

Countess DuVaye stepped back from the row of sinks, putting a hand across her chest as if in pain. In a dramatic voice, she lectured, "My dear, Lady Bianca would never—"

"I believe," Lady Bianca cut in, "the Countess is politely suggesting you consult an Italian dictionary. You must have misunderstood us."

"No, I don't believe I did. And do you know what?" Jennifer took one of the neatly folded towels from the countertop and dried her hands slowly, then turned and lifted her chin, meeting Lady Bianca's icy stare with one of her own. "You're absolutely right about the fact that I'm an American and a commoner. But I'm far better off than you. For all your money and aristocratic heritage, you're nothing more than a weasel."

"A what?" Lady Bianca's eyebrow arched in question. "What, my dear, is a weasel?"

"I suggest *you* consult an *English* dictionary."

With that, Jennifer turned and strode from the ladies' room, keeping her posture every bit as perfect as Lady Bianca's.

Antony forced himself to smile as Bianca approached. Her trips to the powder room never seemed to last as long as he liked. He'd planned to spend the few moments he could snatch between dances conferring with the dean of the Royal San Riminian University. The longtime educator had firm ideas about financing higher education, and Antony wanted to hear the dean's reaction to the scholarship's added service requirement.

Unfortunately, Bianca rarely appreciated his need to engage in serious discussion.

She laced her hand in his arm before he could locate the dean, then looked up at him, her face expectant. "Your Highness, they're about to play the San Riminian Waltz. Shall we?"

How could he say no? He couldn't afford to upset his potential wife. Or, more accurately, his father's belief that she was his potential wife. The dean would have to wait.

Plus, he reminded himself, he enjoyed dancing. And even if he didn't get a chance to speak with the dean himself, Jennifer had probably already engaged him in conversation. He'd simply check with Jennifer to learn the dean's opinions.

With the welcome prospect of speaking to Jennifer in mind, he led Lady Bianca to the floor for the San Riminian Waltz.

As they danced, Antony looked over Bianca's shoulder, scanning the room. Most people were watching him move across the floor, which was nothing new. He'd grown used to the constant attention and whispers over the years. He noticed two photographers, one obviously from San Riminian National News, the other from San Rimini Today, each snapping pictures of him dancing with Lady Bianca. No doubt the shots would appear in the morning newspaper, which would make his father happy.

He smiled to himself. He'd accomplished his goals for the evening. His father would relax, at least for a little while, on the issue of marriage if he thought Antony might marry Lady Bianca. Plus, the press might devote enough attention to the evening's activities to give the San Riminian Scholarship Fund good press coverage.

Finally, and most important, he'd gotten the chance to dance with Jennifer, thanks to Federico. Antony knew memories of their dance—the fruity smell of Jennifer's hair, the soft feel of her dress under his palm, the reflected light from the chandeliers in her blue eyes—would comfort him in the future. If he did end up being forced to marry someone of the aristocracy for the good of the country, he would at least know he'd spent a few moments of his life truly enjoying the company of a woman, engaging in witty banter, savoring the feel of her in his arms.

He looked past the crowd of photographers and admirers, seeking out Jennifer. The sooner he broke away from Lady Bianca and spoke to her about the dean, the better. He couldn't risk having her return to her room for the night before he got the chance to speak with her one last time.

"Who are you looking for, Antony?" Bianca inquired, catching him in the act.

He shrugged, forcing himself to appear disinterested. "Ms. Allen, I suppose. I wanted to be sure to wish her well before she left for the evening."

"I believe she's already gone," Bianca commented. "I saw her earlier in the ladies' room, and...oh, how shall I put this? She said some rather upsetting things to Countess DuVaye." Bianca waved her hand dismissively, "She didn't do it intentionally, of course, but it just wasn't *proper*."

Antony snapped his attention back to Bianca. "What did she say, exactly?"

Lady Bianca shook her head. "Some rather nasty things about San Rimini, I'm afraid. Something about how our accent is ridiculous and can't be understood easily, even by those who speak Italian. You know how patriotic Countess DuVaye can be. She took it rather hard."

"And Ms. Allen simply took her leave after...after disparaging our language?"

"I'm not certain. However, I'm sure once she realized what she'd said, she left the ballroom. I would have. It's a slap in the face to our nation to say such things! Of course," she squeezed his hand, as if to emphasize her point, "you know how patriotic I am. I would never do anything to belittle our nation or its royal family."

"I'm certain you wouldn't." But Jennifer wouldn't either, would she? He couldn't envision it.

"You know," she continued, "I hope one day to be part of the royal family, if it's not too forward of me to say so—"

"Lady Bianca," Antony interrupted, "I need to attend to some important state business. I apologize for cutting our dance short, but it is urgent. As a patriot, I'm sure you understand?''

"Of course," she replied, though a look of disappointment passed over her face.

"Thank you," he managed, then left the dance floor as quickly as he could. He sensed he'd only gotten half the story from Lady Bianca, and he fully intended to learn the rest.

Antony wandered through the crowd, stopping to greet his guests only as long as absolutely necessary before moving on, all the while keeping his eyes open for Jennifer. After a few minutes, he concluded she'd either stayed in the powder room or left the ballroom.

"Federico," he grabbed his brother's elbow, easing him away from a crowd of dignitaries. Careful to keep his voice low, he asked, "Have you seen Ms. Allen?"

"Walking toward the east wing staircase about five minutes ago."

"Heading for her room?"

"I'm not sure," Federico replied slowly, his eyes taking on a what's-this-all-about cast. "Does she know her way?"

That thought hadn't occurred to him. "That's why I need to find her," he improvised. "Sophie is supposed to escort her back to the room at midnight, but Ms. Allen obviously forgot. Don't want to upset Sophie's schedule."

Federico arched an eyebrow. "Right. You pulled me away from the president of the San Riminian Arts Council and two members of parliament to keep from upsetting Sophie?"

"Never mind," Antony waved off his nosy brother, then turned and hurried out of the ballroom, toward the east staircase. Luckily, none of the guests milling about in the hall tried to corner him, hoping to converse with their crown prince.

He took the east stairs in twos, then jogged the length of three hallways to his private wing of the palace. He knocked on Jennifer's door and waited.

No answer.

He knocked again, but no sound came from inside the room. His breath came out in a whoosh. He hadn't even realized he'd been holding it.

Maybe she hadn't left the dinner after all. Then again, perhaps she simply didn't know her way back to her room.

He retraced his steps, looking into the side hallways one by one, hoping for a glimpse of Jennifer. No luck.

He was almost back to the ballroom when he finally saw her.

She stood at the top of the east stairs, as if deciding where she wanted to go. She didn't see him approach. Instead, she turned and walked toward the hallway leading to the king's chambers.

"You don't want to go that way," he called out.

"Why not?"

"About a half dozen guards will stop you."

She turned to face him then, and he was surprised to see her cheeks streaked red. She held her fists balled at her sides, but relaxed them as he looked at her, obviously aware of his scrutiny. A lump rose in his throat. He'd never seen Jennifer upset, and imagined she didn't ruffle easily. What had Lady Bianca done to upset Jennifer so much?

Whatever happened between the two women, he wanted to repair the damage. He knew he shouldn't be so bothered, but he couldn't help himself. He hated the thought that Jennifer wasn't enjoying herself. She, of all people, deserved the chance to get out and enjoy herself at a party once in a while.

"Then I take it that's not the way back to my room, Your Highness?"

"No."

"Would you care to direct me?"

"Only if you tell me what happened in the ladies' room."

Jennifer arched an eyebrow. "Lady Bianca didn't give you the blow-by-blow?"

"I would rather hear your version of events," he stepped forward and took her hand. He wanted to massage all the pent-up anger out of her, wanted to see her back to her calm, rational self. Running his fingers along hers, he continued, "I do not see any bruises, so I assume blow-by-blow is not a literal description of what happened?"

"No," the calm in her voice sounded forced. "Nothing that bad."

"Then what?"

"Prince Antony, I really can't..." she looked up at him, but when her blue eyes met his, she hesitated, as if unsure how she should answer.

He helped her, "On occasion, Lady Bianca and her friends can be rather...rather *rude,* to put it bluntly. You will not offend me by telling the truth, Jennifer."

"If you find them rude, why are they your friends?"

He had to think about that one. It had never occurred to him *not* to have them as friends, since their families had known each other for so many generations. He shrugged. "I do not always approve of their actions. But sometimes, as crown prince, I am compelled to spend time with people I might not befriend were I in any other position. Unfortunately, I have no choice.''

She flexed her hand in his, then looked down at their interlaced fingers. Without pulling away, she said softly, ''We all have choices.''

''Alas, I do not. Not in where I travel, whom I associate with, even in whom I marry. These matters are not so simple for a prince. Even though I am an adult, I am subject to my father's authority as king. And I am subject to the will of the San Riminian people.''

She looked back up at him, bolder now, with a challenge lighting her eyes. ''You *do* have choices, whether you think you do or not. You just aren't willing to live with the consequences.''

He stared at her a moment, unwilling to break the connection forming between them. He'd never before considered consequences. He'd simply done what he'd been told to do his whole life, without question. He'd attended all the right functions, agreed to all the right interviews, selected all the right friends. He'd even been willing to go along with his father's command that he marry a proper bride. But he hadn't done those things because he *wanted* to do them. And he certainly hadn't weighed the consequences of *not* doing them, besides the obvious repercussion of having his subjects believe he didn't deserve to wear their crown.

''You are right, Jennifer,'' he finally whispered. ''I *can* choose. I simply have to live with the consequences.''

And there was one choice he'd been dying to make all night.

With an unexplainable urgency driving him, he pulled Jennifer to him. Tilting her chin, he kissed her, tentatively at first, then more passionately as she responded to him, slowly raising her arms and wrapping them around his shoulders.

Yes. *This* was his choice.

He wanted, if only for a brief moment, to savor the experience of holding a woman who didn't want him simply for his title or his money. Who didn't care if he was a prince, but who possessed the strength of character to question his personal ideas and dreams, making him a better man for the experience.

He ran a hand over her sweet-smelling hair, then pulled her tight against his body. Deepening their kiss, he allowed his tongue to move over her moist lips and savor the taste of her. When she slowly parted her lips and moved her exquisite body against his in response, he was shocked by the wave of desire that rocked through him. In all his years of squiring women around to balls, the obligatory kiss good-night had never come close to matching this one.

Then again, nothing about kissing Jennifer was obligatory.

As he moved his lips down her neck, hungry to taste more of her, a flash of light caught his attention. He tried to ignore it, but then, as hushed conversation floated to his ears from the bottom of the staircase, he realized what it had to be.

Cameras.

Antony jerked back from her as if he'd been slapped. Looking down the staircase, he saw that guests were hurrying out of the ballroom to see what was happening on the stairs. He turned back to Jennifer, who stepped away from him as if in a daze. Her mouth looked pouty and swollen from his kisses, her carefully applied lipstick all but gone.

"Antony?" her voice cracked as she looked from the crowd of guests and photographers, to him, then back to the crowd again.

"No, Jennifer, I did not mean to…"

But his words came too late. Jennifer looked beyond him, spotting Sophie just as the secretary emerged from the hallway leading to his private quarters. Sophie's mouth hung open, but she quickly recovered and ushered Jennifer toward the hall.

Without meeting his eyes, Jennifer ran past Antony and disappeared down the long marble corridor.

Chapter Seven

"Jennifer Allen! Why in the world didn't you tell me?" Pia waved a two-day-old copy of San Rimini Today as she entered the trailer. "It's bad enough we get the newspapers so late, if we even get them at all. But when the scoop of the year is sitting right in front of me, I expect her to tell me about it!"

Jennifer cringed as she set aside the requisition report she'd been preparing for the Rasovo Relief Society's board of directors. Ever since she'd flown home, she'd been trying to get Antony—and the memory of his searing kisses—out of her mind. Burying herself in requisitions hadn't helped. And obviously, hiding out in her office wouldn't help, either.

Jennifer took the newspaper from Pia, and her jaw nearly hit the dusty trailer floor. There, splashed across the front page, was a large picture of her and Antony wrapped in each other's arms.

From the angle of the photo, there was no doubt

this was a more-than-friendly kiss. Even worse, the headline trumpeted:

Antony Raises Money, Lowers His Guard!
San Rimini's Crown Prince Enjoys Amorous
"Pitch" by American Fundraiser

Jennifer put a hand to her stomach as it lurched. How could this be happening?

"This is terrible," she mumbled, still not believing the headline. The newspaper portrayed her as nothing more than a lovesick golddigger. Hadn't her parents warned her over and over about aristocrats and politicians? *Say one thing, do another.* She could almost hear her mother's disappointed words when yet another promise of funds had come up short, like the time a politician offered funding for her parents' Cambodian refugee project if her parents would support his senatorial campaign, but then backed off his promise once he was elected.

Antony's promise of help had come up short in the worst way yet.

"So it's not a doctored photo? Prince Antony actually *kissed* you?" Pia's eyes grew wide. "I certainly wouldn't call that terrible!"

"Did you read the article?"

"The picture isn't enough? I saw it and came running in here as fast as I could."

Jennifer groaned out loud as she scanned the piece. "They're saying that I roped him into kissing me. Apparently, 'sources close to the prince' say that I threw myself at him all night, trying to get publicity for the Rasovo Relief Society, and obviously, trying to get something more for myself!"

"That's not true," Pia protested. "Everyone knows you'd never do that. But does it really matter? I want to hear about this kiss! How'd it happen?"

Jennifer swallowed. The kiss. She couldn't even begin to think about the kiss itself.

"The kiss was nothing, just…just him being polite," she replied. Shaking the newspaper, she continued, "But *this,* this matters a lot," Jennifer closed her eyes for a moment, then opened them to look out her office window at the camp she'd come to know as home.

A group of refugees made their way out of the mess tent, savoring loaves of warm bread—a treat, given the time and manpower it took to make fresh bread for the whole camp. They'd never know the grace and opulence of a royal palace. All they cared about were the simple things, like finding their missing relatives. Having a warm place to sleep. Knowing they'd have a meal and something to quench their thirst at the end of each day.

Jennifer gestured toward the window. "In the end, it matters to them the most, Pia. They won't have confidence in my ability to help them if they think I'm spending my time gallivanting with some hotshot prince instead of fighting for their well-being. They've got a lot of their hopes pinned on me and how I portray them to the rest of the world, and this will devastate them. "

Pia harrumphed. "They know you better than that. Still, if it's any consolation, I don't think they've seen the paper yet. A Red Cross worker loaned me this copy. And there hasn't been mention of it on the radio."

"Well, I guess that's something to be thankful

for.'' She laid the paper out on her desk and wondered
how many people had read the paper—or worse, believed every word of the article.

"Shoot, Pia," she smacked the paper, "I hadn't
even thought of it, but what happens when potential
donors and volunteers read this tripe? They'll assume
I don't take this camp and its mission seriously. Then
they won't take it seriously, either. My whole trip—
the time away from camp, my work preparing the
speech, everything—will have been for nothing.
Worse, I might have actually harmed our cause!''

Pia ran a hand over her short blond hair, looking
as frustrated as Jennifer felt. "Maybe you can call the
paper. Try to have a retraction printed. I'll call my
cousin, Viscount Renati, and tell him what really happened. He might be able to rein in some of the gossip,
and he could talk up the scholarship fund to his
wealthier friends.''

Jennifer skimmed the article again. She had no
doubt as to the identity of the "sources close to the
prince.'' She'd obviously angered those so-called
sources enough during their ladies' room confronta-
tion for the socialites to take their gossip public. She
doubted Pia's cousin stood a chance against the wag-
ging tongues of Lady Bianca and Countess DuVaye.

"No," she finally told Pia. "If I try to talk to the
paper, they'll twist my words. And I won't put your
cousin in an awkward position. The best I can do is
stay out of sight and let the palace deal with it.''

Not that they would. She could still hear Antony's
words after the photographers started shooting. *No,
Jennifer,* he'd said. *I did not mean to...*

Hadn't meant to get caught, she wondered, or
hadn't meant to kiss her at all? Federico *did* say an-

other woman had moved Antony's heart. For all she knew, Antony had even corroborated the story before it went to print. And why wouldn't he? He'd been made out as the good guy, and she'd been depicted as an ''amorous'' fundraiser. Plus, if he did love another woman, as Federico suspected, this version of events would keep him out of hot water with her.

Jennifer exhaled, upset with herself for being so naive. Antony's friends might've been convinced he'd changed, but now that she'd had a couple of days to stew, she didn't think so. Her parents had been right all along. You couldn't trust politicians to do what was right. You could only trust them to do what made them look good to the public.

She reached down to pull on her work boots, which she'd kicked off under the desk when she'd started working on the requisition forms. Suddenly, she craved fresh air. Needed to feel like she was doing something constructive, not simply letting fate control her. ''Let's go outside, Pia,'' she suggested. ''I'd like to take another water sample from the river and one from our purification tanks. Make sure we're keeping it potable.''

Pia frowned. ''I tested them both the day before yesterday. I'm sure the water's fine. Wouldn't you rather figure out this whole Prince Antony mess?''

''What's to figure out?'' she shrugged as she finished lacing her boots. ''I'm never going to see him again, so it doesn't matter. Now let's hurry and get those water samples.''

''I expect this behavior from Stefano, but not from you,'' Federico hissed over the coffee, bacon, mushroom omelets and hot buttered toast that comprised their traditional San Riminian Sunday breakfast. "I'm surprised you were brave enough to come to breakfast this morning, after avoiding Father all day yesterday." Federico shook his head. "I don't understand. How could you let yourself get caught kissing Jennifer Allen?"

Antony ignored his brother. The two princes sat alone in the cavernous palace dining room, but both brothers knew King Eduardo would join them at the breakfast-laden oak table any minute.

"Antony? I will not let you ignore me. I am your brother, and your behavior affects me as well."

Antony shot his brother an angry look. In the thirty-six hours since the incriminating photograph hit the newsstands, he'd been second-guessing himself more than Federico ever could. Having Federico berate his behavior, especially after he'd gotten an earful from Lady Bianca, didn't help matters.

"Okay," Federico whispered, afraid as Antony was that the staff—or worse, the king—might overhear them. "I concede that Ms. Allen is good-looking and intelligent. She has a wonderful sense of humor. And I think she has affected your heart as no woman before. I like her immensely. But you cannot go on like this."

Antony wiped his lips with his napkin, wishing Federico would let the Jennifer issue rest. Unfortunately, he knew his father would have even more to say, and would say it less democratically than his brother.

Federico glanced toward the doors to the kitchen, making sure no staff members were lingering. Obviously unwilling to let up on the topic, he whispered, "I want you to be happy as much as anyone, Antony.

But it is not our lot in life. You know you are duty-bound to marry a noblewoman like Bianca and produce heirs, even if you're infatuated with someone else.''

''I choose not to.''

Federico blinked. After a moment's recovery, he argued, ''You *choose* not to? Our position does not allow us to choose. Father arranged my marriage to Lucrezia, and it has worked out for the best, despite my initial misgivings. We have produced two heirs. The match is good for San Rimini.''

Antony put his napkin down, then pushed back from the table. ''But is it good for you, Federico?'' he asked quietly. ''Are you happy? Have you ever thought there might be more to life than this?'' he waved his hand at the valuable artwork that filled the room, ''or this?'' He held up his hand, indicating one of the rings passed down to each San Riminian crown prince over the country's long history.

Federico sighed. ''No. And I do not think about it. *This* is the role we were born to, and I've come to accept that. As much as you might want to be with Ms. Allen, and as much as I wish it were possible for you, it's not. If you don't accept that fact now, Father will force you to soon.''

''Well, I want more for myself. I want to be a better person here,'' he tapped his chest. ''Jennifer makes me a better person.''

''I realize that. And so does anyone else who watched you at dinner that night. But surely you can find someone who—''

The main doors to the dining room swung open, the hinges creaking with the weight of the heavy oak.

King Eduardo strode in, stopping short when he saw Antony standing beside the table.

"Federico, would you kindly allow me to speak with your brother in private?"

Federico glanced at Antony, then stood. The brothers both knew King Eduardo hadn't been making a request, but a command. "Of course, Father. Perhaps you could join Lucrezia and me for dinner tonight?"

"Perhaps."

Federico nodded, then left the room, leaving Antony alone with his father for the first time since the ballroom fiasco.

The furrow lines in the king's brow ran deeper than usual as he stared at Antony. "You have been avoiding me, my son. According to Sophie, you have been indisposed when I have wished to speak with you."

"Yes, Father. But I am here now."

The king turned slowly, apparently suffering pain despite faithfully taking his medication, then closed the doors to the dining room before taking a seat at the table and gesturing for Antony to do the same.

"I have used the time to contemplate your actions, Antony. I approve of your indiscretion no more now than I did when I was awakened and told of it Friday night. However, I have had time to collect my thoughts on the matter, and have a plan."

Antony nodded, unwilling to say anything to worsen the situation. His father tended to have a temper, and Antony knew he was doing his best to rein it in. He wasn't ready to risk giving his father a heart attack by arguing over whatever his "plan" might be.

The king ran a hand over his salt-and-pepper hair. "Have you reviewed your schedule for this week, Antony?"

"Yes, sir."

"Are you occupied on Wednesday?"

He'd hoped to go to Haffali and apologize to Jennifer, if Giulio could still swing the often-dangerous flight. But he wasn't about to confess that to his father. "I am available if the matter is an important one. Why?"

"Since I assume, given your behavior at the fundraiser on Friday night, that Lady Bianca is no longer speaking to you..." he looked to Antony for confirmation.

"You assume correctly." Not that he really cared, though he knew he should. For nearly a year, he'd been doing his best to find something to love in Bianca. His brother did have a point—a marriage to Bianca would be a good match for San Rimini. Yet, deep in his heart, he found little to like in her, let alone to love.

He focused his attention back on his father. "However, I am not sure she'll accept an apology at this point, if that is what you have planned."

"On the contrary. I have arranged for Countess Benedetta and her daughter, Lady Francesca, to pay our family a visit Wednesday evening. We will have dinner in the formal dining room. Afterward, while I speak with the Countess, please show Lady Francesca the grounds. Talk to her. Get to know her."

So this was what calmed his father's mind. Matchmaking. But Antony wasn't about to acknowledge his suspicion. "Why, Father? What business do you have with the Countess?"

"Not the sort you envision." The king leaned across the table, forcing Antony to meet his gaze. "My son, unless you have a more suitable match in mind, I want you to marry Lady Francesca in no less than one year. I will be working with her mother on Wednesday night to arrange it.''

"Father!" Antony couldn't believe it. His father had never even met Lady Francesca. And he'd only met her himself, what, three times in his life? He knew nothing about the woman, save that she was the daughter of a Countess and had studied art history at the Sorbonne in Paris. That wasn't enough to build a marriage on, not unless he wanted a marriage devoid of love like Federico's.

"You left me no choice, Antony."

"No choice." Antony gritted his teeth, forcing himself not to upset his fragile father. Why did everyone seem to think there were no choices in life? He thought again of Jennifer. In the past few days, she'd challenged his thinking as no woman ever had.

He wondered what she thought of his choice to kiss her—and its consequences—now. Probably nothing pleasant, of that much he was certain. And she'd think even worse things if she heard of his engagement to Francesca Benedetta.

King Eduardo pushed back from the table. "My surgery is scheduled for two weeks from today. I expect to have the engagement announced and this— this *issue* settled before then. It is of utmost importance. Am I understood, son?"

"Yes, sir. But I do so under protest."

"Fine." The king stood, grabbed a piece of toast from the middle of the table, then headed for the door.

Antony let out a deep breath. So much for choices. And for their consequences. He'd done his best to wiggle out from his father's ultimatum, but he'd only succeeded in making matters worse.

Much worse.

"And Antony?" The king turned just as he reached the door and leveled a look of warning at his eldest son. "You are to have no further contact with Ms. Allen. If you feel the need to visit Rasovo regarding your scholarship fund, you are to send Federico or Stefano in your place. You may not see her again."

Fury rolled through Antony's gut, enough to make him leap out of his chair to argue, despite his father's ill health. How dare his father forbid him from seeing Jennifer entirely? He was a grown man and had certain freedoms, for goodness sake, even if his father *was* the king of San Rimini.

He tried to calm himself, but couldn't completely rein in his anger with his father and the adolescent way he was being treated, despite the situation. "Father, I must protest. The fund—"

The king held up a hand, and the look on his face spoke volumes. "You and I both know this is not simply about the San Riminian Scholarship Fund. You will remain here, in the royal palace, until your engagement to Lady Francesca is officially announced. There will be no debate."

Antony flipped the leather-bound book he'd been reading closed, then stared out the window of his private apartments toward the sprawling royal gardens. The sun's early morning rays tipped the flowers and trees with gold, heralding the arrival of another day. A few robins flicked from tree to tree, and a squirrel bolted across a swath of open lawn. To Antony, they seemed impossibly free.

He stood and yanked the heavy royal blue silk curtains closed. He didn't care to think about the animals and their freedom for yet another sunrise.

Turning, he faced his empty bed. It remained, for the third morning in a row, just as the maid had prepared it for him the evening before. The sheets had been carefully turned down, the pillows fluffed, and a crystal glass and fresh bottle of water had been placed on the nightstand.

To anyone else, the rich down comforter and luxuriously soft sheets might seem inviting. However, Antony had preferred to sit in his deep leather chairs and read the nights away, hoping to take his mind off his scheduled dinner with Lady Francesca on Wednesday.

And off Jennifer.

If he'd allowed himself to lie in the bed, he'd only be able to think of what would happen if he had to accept his fate and share it with Francesca, when what he really wanted was to share it with Jennifer, to awaken with the sheets rumpled from a night of slow, worshipful lovemaking....

His plan to distract himself hadn't worked, of course. The same thoughts had flooded his mind even as he sat across the room, alone in his chair. How could they not, after the sensuous kiss they'd shared?

Exasperated, Antony tossed the book—the same Dickens classic he'd opened and stared at every night since his father's pronouncement—onto the scrupulously arranged bed. Three nights and he'd only read to page fifty.

Running a hand over his stubbly chin, Antony headed for the corner armoire. Maybe the morning news would get his mind back on the business of being crown prince to a proud country. Then he'd shave, shower and try to meet the day refreshed. If he managed to shake the cobwebs from his brain, maybe he could even figure out a way to delay his fate until after his father's surgery, when he might be able to convince the man to consider other possibilities.

After opening the antique armoire's pocket doors to reveal a small television, Antony grabbed the remote and returned to his leather chair. Flipping to the San Riminian National News station, he waited through five minutes of commercials before the immense grandfather clock near his door struck the top of the hour, signaling the beginning of the morning broadcast.

He yawned through the reports on oil prices and the American stock market, which usually held him spellbound as he worked on his plans for San Rimini's economic future. Once the news turned to foreign affairs, though, Antony finally began to perk up, and he found himself paying closer attention to news of internal conflicts in Russia, parliamentary reforms in Britain and the American presidential campaigns.

Then a picture popped on the screen that knocked the wind out of his chest in a rush. Rasovo.

The voiceover noted, "Today, rebel conflicts in Rasovo have moved closer to the San Riminian border. Though our nation remains out of danger as the government forces work to defeat the last of the rebels, errant bombs triggered several rockslides in the remote border areas of Rasovo. As you see from these aerial pictures, it has become impossible to reach several of the mountain villages and refugee camps. Local roads are buried under boulders and other debris, and aid has been cut off—''

"Jennifer," he whispered to himself.

The reporter went on to speculate that once the rebels moved out of the area, which they seemed to be doing, there might be a way to get aid to the Rasovars. "Until then, the loss of life and property will remain uncertain," she concluded.

The broadcast turned to another topic, and Antony quickly punched buttons on his remote control, surfing the foreign stations until he found another report on the Rasovar fighting. Like the first report, this one was done from the air. And like the first report, the news agency would only say that there were "unconfirmed" reports of casualties among civilians, but that no numbers could be ascertained until outside relief reached the area.

Desperate for more information, Antony flipped stations, but the news programs were wrapping up.

"Damn!" he yelled to himself.

He had to know if Jennifer was okay. If she was even alive. How could his father possibly stop him from seeing Jennifer now? Antony groaned aloud. He couldn't possibly raise the issue with his father, given his delicate health.

He flew out of his chair, infuriated enough to punch holes in the pristinely-papered walls. He'd never before felt helpless, and he didn't intend to stay helpless anymore.

I'm the crown prince of San Rimini, he thought angrily. I have to do *something,* royal command to stay within the palace walls or not.

A knock sounded at his door, but Antony ignored it. If it was Sophie, he didn't need her to know his plans. It would only put her in an awkward position when his father came to her demanding to know his whereabouts.

He strode back to his dressing room, then grabbed a Louis Vuitton duffel bag from the top shelf. Spinning around, he stared at the freshly-pressed contents of his backlit dressing room closet. What did one take when traveling on a rescue mission through dangerous territory? Certainly not a suit and tie. Or polished loafers. He grabbed one of the few long-sleeved T-shirts he owned and stuffed it in the bag, then began searching for the hiking boots he usually wore at his family's country estate.

"You'll need to be more subtle than that." The familiar voice behind him nearly shocked him into dropping the duffel bag.

"Where have you been since Thursday?" Antony managed to recover, turning to face Stefano, knowing his younger brother had simply strolled into his chambers when Antony refused to answer his knock. "And what makes you think you can invade my privacy?"

Stefano waved a hand. "I went on an impromptu ski trip. Since I didn't notify my secretary of my whereabouts, I'm quite certain I'll hear about it once Father discovers I've returned. However," Stefano dropped his athletic body into a chair in the corner of the dressing room, "in the meantime, I thought you might need my expert advice."

Antony snorted. "Advice from you? About what, I cannot imagine."

"If you want to escape the palace unseen, you certainly aren't going to ask Federico or Isabella how to do it, are you?"

Antony looked down at the half-filled duffel in his hand. So Stefano had seen the morning news, as well.

No doubt his younger brother's instinct told him, given the recent headlines regarding Jennifer, that Antony would go to her. Antony wasn't usually so rash, but for the towheaded Stefano "rash" seemed an everyday happening.

Antony turned back to his dressing room drawers and continued filling his bag, hoping Stefano would give up. But Stefano simply made a show of folding his arms across his chest and leaning back in the chair, refusing to leave.

After grabbing a pair of thick socks from the top drawer, Antony muttered, "Fine. What is your so-called expert advice, Stef?"

"If you plan to go to Rasovo, you cannot simply march through the royal palace with a packed designer bag. Trust me, Father will know before you even make it outside your apartments."

"You suggest I pack no clothes? No toiletries?"

"As the Americans say, *bingo.*"

Antony laughed. "You must be joking." But even as he said it, he knew Stefano was right. His brother had probably learned a thing or two during his brief time in the San Riminian army.

"You aren't exactly going to a polo party, Antony. You're entering a war zone. Call ahead to Giulio. Tell him to load the helicopter with all the food, water, rope and first aid supplies he can find. And tell him to do it on the quiet."

Antony shook his head. "Please tell me you don't involve Giulio in your schemes? He would never—"

"You clearly don't know your own helicopter pilot, because he most certainly would. How do you think I got to Zermatt this weekend? Not on the bus."

Antony leaned back against the dressing room wall.

"Well. I never thought about it before. But, on this *rare* occasion, perhaps you are correct." And if it would help Jennifer, or the people of the Haffali camp, he was willing to gamble on Stefano's experience.

The two men strode back into Antony's bedroom. Antony grabbed the telephone to call Giulio, then set the receiver back down in its cradle as a thought occurred to him. "Do you have a cell phone with you, Stefano?"

Stefano grinned and whipped one out of his pocket. "I suppose you old men can be taught. The last thing you want to do is go through the palace switchboard."

Antony grabbed the cell phone and dialed the number for the helicopter pilot. "Thanks. But I am not an old man," he pointed out to Stefano. "I am only thirty-four."

Stefano was about to argue, but Antony held up a hand to stop him as Giulio's voice crackled in his ear. He explained his dilemma to the pilot and, to his surprise, found Giulio only too willing to help.

"We may need to discuss this later, Giulio," Antony threatened. "Sneaking around behind King Eduardo's back to honor his sons' wishes is risky business. And I understand this isn't the first time."

Giulio laughed. "We can talk at length, Your Highness, so long as we make it in and out of Rasovo in one piece." His voice turned serious, "I'll caution you, if the news reports are true, we might not be able to land. We also risk being shot by the rebels as they retreat from the mountains. You put yourself in grave danger trying to fly into Haffali today."

Antony took a deep breath. "It's a risk we have to

take, Giulio. The Rasovar people are our neighbors and have been friends of San Rimini for centuries. Helping them is the duty of the San Riminian royal family.''

And helping Jennifer was his *personal* duty. He owed it to her, after the scene he made at the fund-raising dinner. Besides, even if he could never marry her, he couldn't live with the knowledge that she might be hurt, or worse, when he could do something to help.

Because whether it was proper or not, he'd fallen in love with her.

Certainly his father would understand, if he explained that the Rasovars needed him, so long as he returned for dinner with Lady Francesca as planned. Even if he hadn't completely figured out how to postpone their engagement until his father was well enough to listen to reason.

He buried the thought as Guilio's voice came on the line again.

''Be at the helipad in an hour,'' the pilot instructed, ''and I'll have water and rescue supplies loaded and ready to go.''

''I'll be there,'' he replied, then gave a thumbs-up to Stefano.

Antony only hoped he wasn't too late.

Chapter Eight

Jennifer swiped dirt off her face with the back of her hand, then tried for the third time to force the smallest of the boulders off the hospital wall.

Or, more correctly, what *used* to be the hospital wall.

When the last bomb hit the nearby hillside, the resulting slide of rocks and debris caused the temporary building's thin wooden walls to come crashing down and its canvas roof to collapse in, leaving patients and staff in the children's section trapped underneath.

Jennifer shook out her arms, trying to relieve some of the muscle ache. Even using a wooden lever she'd fashioned from a broken tent pole, the rock barely budged. How could she possibly get into the collapsed section of the hospital when the stupid rocks weighed so much?

"Pia," she called over the screams of the children still trapped inside, "Pia!"

"Back here," Pia's exhausted voice came from behind the collapsed tent. "I found some exposed canvas I can cut into…I think I can get the rest of the kids out through the hole. It looks like they're all going to be okay!"

Jennifer exhaled, her breath coming out in a loud *whoosh* as she let go of the pole. She just needed to know the kids survived the rockslide. In her mind, she'd pictured the worst.

She ran around to the back of the hospital, thankful that the large rockslide had missed all but the children's end of the makeshift ward.

The adult patients were long ago safely evacuated to the mess tent, along with most of the children. According to the head count, however, at least eight children and a nurse were still trapped. The freed patients wanted to help, but Jennifer was afraid they'd reinjure themselves by straining to move the splintered wood and heavy rocks, let alone the fact that too many people digging in too many places around the trapped children could trigger an even worse collapse.

After reaching the rear of the tent, Jennifer crouched in front of the hole Pia had created in the canvas roof. A nurse still trapped in the hospital urged the children through the opening, while Pia lifted them out, placing them safely onto litters headed for the mess tent and their worried parents.

Jennifer dusted off a little girl and, finding her uninjured, pointed her down the hill toward the mess tent, finally hopeful that the children had all survived.

Suddenly, the ground shook with all the power of an earthquake. Jennifer grabbed for one of the nearby boulders to steady herself, but missed and hit the ground hard.

"Duck down! Cover your heads!" she yelled to the children. "Get down!"

Once the ground stopped shaking from the nearby explosion, she watched as the little girl she'd just helped sprinted for the mess tent. Turning, she crawled to the tent opening and called to the nurse over the sound of the children's cries, "How many more?"

"Seven."

"Try to keep them calm, but hurry. We've got to get them out in case those bombs cause another slide."

Six children later, the petite nurse poked her head out the opening. Shielding her eyes from the bomb's dust, she said, "I've still got Josef in here. His bed flipped when the rockslide started, and there are some rocks on top of it. He seems fine, but I'm afraid I'm not strong enough to lift the bed off him."

Jennifer gestured to Pia. "Run around front and grab that hunk of wood I was using for a lever."

Focusing on the nurse, she instructed, "C'mon out. The doctors will need your help tending the injured. I'll free Josef and be along in a moment."

Jennifer offered her hand to the nurse, helping the blonde navigate through the rocks and the small hole in the canvas.

Once the nurse emerged into the daylight, she brushed the dust off her usually clean scrubs. Her face and arms bore fresh scratches from the rocks she'd scraped against on the way out.

"Boy, that was tight," she blinked. "Good thing I got stuck instead of Nurse Tindall. I don't think she'd have fit through there."

"I may have a hard time myself," Jennifer admitted, taking her flashlight from where she'd stuck it in the back of her waistband then shining it into the gap. "Wish me luck."

"Want me to wait?"

"Nah, go on ahead. The kids in the mess tent will be looking for you, besides the fact that the doctors will need you. With all the scrapes the patients sustained, you'll have your hands full trying to clean them up and prevent infections. Pia is here to help me if I get stuck."

The nurse nodded just as Pia rounded the corner of the collapsed tent, pole in hand. "Just be careful, Jennifer," the nurse warned. "With all the rocks and broken furniture, it's cramped in there. The canvas from the tent roof will be right on your head, and the tent frame was completely smashed. The splintered pieces are sharp and hard to see, even with a flashlight. Plus, there's broken glass everywhere—"

Jennifer waved her off. "I get the idea. I don't plan to be inside long. Just be sure to tell Josef's mother that he's going to be all right. I had a hard time convincing her to wait for us in the mess tent, and if she sees you come back without him—"

"Got it." She nodded at Pia, then jogged down the hill.

Pia crouched at the opening as Jennifer lowered herself to the ground and crawled through the canvas. Once through the hole, her shoulders grazed rocks on both sides of the narrow gap, and she found herself having to stretch her arms in front of her and grab indentations on the rocks to move her body forward into the main area of the collapsed tent. After two long minutes of pulling herself through the tight space, she finally reached the main section of the tent.

"Josef!" she called, trying to get her bearings.

"I here, Miss Jennifer!" His voice sounded frightened, but strong. "I hold on for you!"

Jennifer turned back to grab the lever as Pia threaded it through the small hole she'd just entered through. Once she had the pole, she used it to push up against the canvas so she could shine her flashlight around the room. She forced back a lump in her throat. All their months of work on the hospital were down the drain. Little worth salvaging remained. She comforted herself with the thought that, despite the damage, at least no one had died as a result of the bombing or the rockslides. And with the rebels cornered, hopefully the civil war would be over soon.

Aiming her flashlight toward the area where Josef's bed used to be, she called out for him again.

"Here! Here!" came his reply.

Jennifer turned toward his voice, then picked her way through the collapsed tent until she located the boy. As the nurse indicated, his bed had flipped upside down in the slide. A large section of the wooden tent wall and several rocks rested on top of it, and the glass from a nearby cabinet door lay shattered on the floor all around. Josef smiled up at her from the floor.

"This one big mess, Miss Jennifer. But I will be A-okay."

She couldn't help but grin. Josef's optimistic words were the first cheerful ones she'd heard all day.

"Of course you'll be A-okay, Josef. How's the leg?" She kept talking as she took the lever and wedged it under the bed.

Josef cringed as Jennifer shifted the bed. "It hurt very much. But I also very much tough. Prince Antony tell me I tough!"

The memory of Antony, sitting next to Josef's hospital bed and reading children's stories just two short weeks before, flashed through Jennifer's mind. He'd seemed so honest and giving then, worrying about Josef's leg, and expressing concern about the fact that Josef's family had to hide in the bushes until they could get a ride into the camp.

Would he express that same concern now, given the chance?

The bed creaked, then the rocks shifted enough so Jennifer could lift the bedframe off Josef. Holding the lever with both hands to keep the bed off the little boy's legs, she nodded to the nearby medicine cabinet. "Josef, do you see that cabinet on the ground behind you?"

He twisted his neck to look, then nodded. "You want me to pull cabinet?"

"Yes. Reach behind you and use the cabinet to pull yourself out. But be very careful of the broken glass. Can you do that?"

Josef grinned, his face as proud as any young boy bragging about his strength. "No problem, Miss Jennifer. I can do!"

Jennifer watched while Josef struggled to pull his battered body out from under the bed, encouraging him as he slid along the floor inch by inch. Once his feet cleared the bedframe, Jennifer released the wooden pole, dropping the bed, then went to his side.

"We go now?" he whispered, his voice tinged with fear despite his brave face. "My mother, she will worry."

"We'll have to get you to her right away, then," Jennifer replied. She quickly inspected his wound, then lifted him into her arms as best she could.

She kept talking to Josef as she picked her way back through the tent. His leg was bleeding, but didn't look to be too badly injured. As soon as she got him to the mess tent, the doctors would be able to clean out the wounds and bandage them. In the meantime, she didn't want Josef to panic when he saw the blood.

"Miss Jennifer?" Josef looked up at her, making sure he had her attention. "Prince Antony tell me to come to palace when I better. But what if I not better? Prince Antony mad then, no?"

Jennifer wanted to get out of the collapsed tent as soon as possible, before the army decided to drop another bomb anywhere near the camp, but Josef's question stopped her cold.

"Josef," she adjusted her hold on his small body and looked him square in the eye. "You *will* get better. I promise."

His eyes brightened a little. "Then I go to palace?"

Jennifer's heart sank. How could she tell him no? That she'd foolishly kissed the prince and ruined any hope she had of making Josef's dream come true?

Kicking a piece of broken wood out of their way, she once again moved toward the small exit. "Let's work on getting out of here first, okay, Josef? Then we'll see about going to San Rimini."

"Good." He wrapped his arms around her neck, satisfied for the moment.

Finally, Jennifer found the small hole in the canvas and called up to Pia. "I've got him!"

"I'll pull him up," she called back. Then, suddenly, Pia yelled, "Get down!" at the same time Jennifer heard the buzz of an approaching airplane. As best she could in the cramped space, Jennifer lowered Josef to the floor and covered his body with her own.

"Miss Jennifer?"

"Hang on," she instructed, then held her breath as the plane passed overhead.

The last thing she heard was the earthshaking reverberation of a bomb slamming into the mountainside above her.

Antony held tight to his seat as Giulio circled over the mountains, looking for a safe spot to land the helicopter near the Haffali camp. He could hardly believe his eyes. The damage done by the Rasovar army in an effort to contain retreating rebel forces was evident. The mountain roads, often used by the rebels, were pockmarked with holes from weapons fire and strewn with debris. Small fires burned in abandoned mountain shacks nearby, and a thick blend of smoke and dust filled the air.

"Not quite the same as last time, is it, Your Highness?" Giulio asked as the Haffali camp came into view. "And we thought it was bad then."

Antony didn't even answer as the shock of seeing the camp itself hit him full-force. Although no bombs seemed to have hit the camp directly, three large craters gaped in the hillside above the camp's hospital. The hospital appeared partially collapsed, covered by rocks and dirt from the blown-out hill. He could only imagine how many patients had been trapped inside.

Nearby, a few of the refugees' makeshift tents were also smashed. Clothing, knocked off the thin clotheslines, lay scattered about on the road. A donkey ran through the middle of the mess, and a man limped along behind it before turning and entering the mess tent.

The tanks containing the camp's purified water

were overturned, and a few refugees gathered near the river, taking turns filling their buckets with water muddied by debris. Another group of refugees ran toward the helipad, waving their arms at the chopper, obviously anxious for any help.

Nowhere did he see Jennifer. His stomach knotted as he scoured the landscape, searching for any sign of her fiery red hair among the low, grayish tents or near the river. Was she inside one of the buildings that withstood the bomb blasts? Or dead, somewhere in the rubble?

"Can we land there?" Antony yelled over the engine noise, pointing to the helipad. He had to get down, had to see if Jennifer was all right.

"I think so, Your Highness. But we can't stay long. We'll be sitting ducks if the rebels decide they want the chopper. The helipad's visible for nearly a mile."

"Understood."

Once they were on the ground Antony unbuckled his belt, then turned to gather supplies from behind his seat.

"Once we've got these unloaded, take the helicopter and go back to San Rimini," he instructed. "Have Stefano help you load more supplies, then bring them first thing tomorrow morning."

"Your Highness, I'm not leaving you here—"

He held up his hand to stop Giulio's argument, then realized he probably looked just like his father—holding his hand up to keep from having to listen to others' point of view. The last thing Giulio needed was to be reminded about how angry King Eduardo would be when he discovered what they'd done.

"Giulio," he began again. "There are very few able-bodied men here. By staying, I can help. I will be in no more danger here than you will be flying over land held by the Rasovar rebels.''

"True,'' Giulio answered, but his forehead remained creased with skepticism.

"I shall fly back with you in the morning. By then, the rebels will probably have left the area, and the Red Cross and other relief organizations will have come.''

Giulio shook his head. "Forgive me for saying so, Your Highness. But I never expected you to be so...so involved. You surprise me today.''

Antony rolled a small barrel of water out of the back of the chopper and onto the landing pad. "I surprise myself as well, Giulio.'' As much as he thought he knew the direction of his life, and as much as he thought he knew himself, two weeks ago he never would have predicted he'd be back at Haffali. Especially not working in a war zone, trying to find a gorgeous American woman with no aristocratic roots, and against his father's express orders.

Ten minutes later, after a group of thankful refugees made it to the landing pad and helped unload the helicopter, Antony waved as Giulio took off for San Rimini.

Once the noise of the helicopter faded, he tried asking the refugees about Jennifer. Unfortunately, he spoke only a few words in Rasovar, and few of them spoke Italian or English. They seemed to know what he was asking, but couldn't give him a reply he could understand. And they seemed far more intent on getting the supplies down to the camp than answering questions about Jennifer.

Frustrated, Antony lifted a coil of rope onto his shoulders and grabbed hold of a small wagon with a barrel of fresh water inside. He'd have to help first and ask questions about Jennifer later.

As Antony made his way to the camp with the refugees, a few of them smiled at him and gestured to the water and medical supplies they now carried. He couldn't help but smile back. He now walked the same road he'd seen the refugees take with their over-burdened, dilapidated wagon the first time he'd visited the camp. He'd been stunned by their tired appearance then. And though the road was every bit as dusty and dirty as it had been the first time, and the refugees probably in worse shape, he knew he belonged here.

For the first time in his life, he was doing something that made a difference. Not just raising money. Not asking others to volunteer. But doing the hard work himself.

He had to admit, he enjoyed the feeling. He only hoped he'd get the opportunity to share his revelation with Jennifer soon.

Finally, as they entered the main area of the camp, a doctor he'd met briefly on his tour emerged from one of the small tents, leading a young girl toward the mess tent.

"Excuse me," Antony called to the woman, a British doctor if he remembered correctly. "I am looking for Jennifer Allen. Do you know where she might be?"

The doctor stopped short, and her eyes widened as she recognized Antony. "I—I'm not certain. Some of the staff are setting up a station to distribute fresh water. It's behind the mess tent. Sh-shall I show you, Your Highness?"

Antony smiled, hoping to put the woman at ease.

"I believe I can find it. You have a more important job." He winked at the little girl, thanked the doctor, then turned and pulled the wagon toward the back of the mess tent. Only the weight of the wagon kept him from running. He offered a silent prayer, hoping to find Jennifer working at the water station, all in one piece.

When he turned the corner at the rear of the mess tent, however, he found himself face-to-face with chaos. A member of the Rasovo Relief Society's staff stood on a heavy table, yelling at the top of his lungs for refugees to wait their turn to get fresh water. A nurse he'd seen during his tour tried to herd the frantic refugees into lines, while three men he thought worked in the mess tent hefted a pitifully small barrel of water onto the table, then fiddled with a spigot.

"Only one liter per person," he heard one of the men who'd lifted the barrel tell the others. "Otherwise, there won't be enough for the doctors to use for cleaning instruments and for washing." The three men looked at each other, then at the crowd of refugees desperate for fresh water.

"What should we tell them?" one of them asked.

The first man replied, "That we hope to have more tomorrow or Friday, and to use what they have sparingly. They are not, under any circumstances, to use the river. Not until we can be sure no pollutants entered the supply."

"Easier said than done. If Jennifer were here, they'd listen to her—"

Antony stepped forward. "I brought some fresh water in on my helicopter. My pilot has gone back for more."

The workers turned to look at him, a mixture of

surprise and relief registering on their tired faces. "You're a godsend," the first man finally spoke up. "How you managed to fly in, I don't know. But we sure are grateful."

As two of the workers grabbed the barrel out of Antony's wagon, Antony turned to the man who'd mentioned Jennifer. "You said that Jennifer isn't here. Do you know where she is? Or if she's all right?"

The man took a deep breath. "Quite honestly, we don't know. In case of emergencies, everyone is to meet at the mess tent. She and Pia haven't shown up yet."

Antony's stomach clenched. It wasn't like Jennifer not to follow established procedures. Not unless something awful had happened. He almost hated to ask, "No one has seen her, then? Where was she when the bombing began?"

The staff member who'd been standing on the table jumped down. "I heard a nurse say Jennifer was at the hospital." He jerked his thumb toward the collapsed tent at the base of the hill. "Evacuating children or something. I dunno. Heard it thirdhand. And that was a while ago. She's probably not there anymore. I'd recheck the mess tent."

He let out his breath, relieved to know she'd at least been seen. "Do you know—"

"Help! Please, my son!" A woman pushed her way through the crowd and grabbed the arm of one of the men distributing water. "Please, please, to help! My son trapped in hopp-it-all!"

"I thought everyone was out of there," one of the relief workers piped up. He asked her, "Have you checked in the mess tent?"

"He in hopp-it-all. He stuck. Please!"

Antony nodded to the workers manning the water station. "You have your hands full here. I can help her."

As much as he wanted to find Jennifer, Antony forced himself to bury his thoughts of her for the moment. He had to put this frightened woman's needs before his own, or Jennifer's. Somehow, he knew that's what Jennifer would want him to do.

She pointed to the hillside with her free hand, and he jogged along with her. Antony couldn't help but be concerned as the look on the woman's face grew more desperate.

Finally, they circled to the back of the hospital. Surveying the crushed remnants of the tent, Antony didn't hold out much hope. How could her son have survived?

She looked up at him then, as if he were her only hope in the world. "The hopp-it-all, it fall down. My son Josef in it. Please."

Josef? The little boy he'd met during his visit? His throat constricted. Something about the little boy had touched him, more than he wanted to admit. He laid a calming hand on the woman's shoulder and in Italian, said, "I will find your son. I promise."

She smiled, and he hoped that meant she trusted him. Even if she didn't understand him.

"Prince Antony! Your Highness!"

He tore his gaze away from Josef's mother, searching for the origin of the feminine voice. Finally, he saw Pia crouched at the edge of the tent, waving for him to join her. "Prince Antony! Help me pull Josef out!"

Antony ran to Pia's side. Near her feet, a large

opening had been cut in the tent canvas. Inside, he could just make out Josef, pulling his way through a narrow tunnel of rocks.

"I can reach him," Antony said as he dropped to his stomach in front of Pia.

Working with Pia, he gently pulled Josef free of the rocks.

"Prince Antony!" the little boy breathed once he emerged from the tent. "I much hope you come for me. You come for Miss Jennifer, too?"

Before Antony could ask Josef what he meant, the little boy looked past him, seeing his mother struggling up the hill. "Mamma!"

The woman began crying, then fell to her knees. Pia gently took Josef and placed him in his mother's arms. Returning to Antony's side, she whispered. "Thank you. I'm so glad you came, Your Highness. Your presence will make a big difference to these people. I'm proud to call you my future king." She smiled at him, a genuine smile that warmed his heart, then turned back to the canvas opening and shone her flashlight down the hole.

Antony couldn't help but wonder if Jennifer would be as proud.

He knew he shouldn't care. Knew he should be focused on helping the Rasovars, then on getting home and pursuing his other duties—like marrying Lady Francesca. Still, he couldn't get Jennifer out of his mind.

He took a deep breath. Perhaps the best thing was to find Jennifer, assure himself that she was all right, then head back to San Rimini in the morning.

He laid a hand on Pia's shoulder, urging her to stop looking back into the damaged hospital. "I am sorry.

I doubt it can be salvaged. We should help Josef and his mother to the mess tent,'' he suggested, urging Pia to her feet. ''He needs to have his leg treated. I hope to find Ms. Allen there, as well.''

Pia shook her head. ''You don't understand. Jennifer's not at the mess tent.''

Antony stopped short, a feeling of dread grabbing his gut. ''Where—''

''Still trapped inside. I can see her, but I can't reach her. I'll need your help.''

Before Pia could finish speaking, he grabbed her flashlight from the ground, then shone it through the hole in the canvas. For a moment, he saw nothing but rocks, dirt and splintered wood, but gradually he was able to make out what had once been the hospital floor.

Then his heart nearly stopped. A woman lay across the floor, unmoving. Though she was facedown, he couldn't mistake the red hair splayed across the dirt. *Jennifer.*

He had no idea if she was dead or alive.

Chapter Nine

Antony. She'd been dreaming about Antony.

Jennifer raised her head, then realized where she was. Not safely in her trailer, tucked in her cot, but in the collapsed hospital.

She looked around the dusty interior for a moment, trying to get her bearings. The opening Pia had cut in the canvas had to be nearby. She simply needed to locate the passageway through the rocks leading there…get Josef out…

Josef.

The thought hit her like a tent pole to the stomach. Josef had been with her. And his leg had been bleeding. Where was he now?

"Josef?" she croaked out, her mouth parched. "Josef?"

"Josef is up here, Jennifer. We have him."

Jennifer blinked a few times, then dropped her aching head back to the dusty ground. She had to have a head injury. Had to be hearing things. The voice sounded so much like Antony's, even the heavily accented *"Zhennifer."*

"Jennifer? Are you all right?"

She swallowed hard. How long had she been trapped inside the hospital? At the fundraising dinner, Federico told her Antony believed in her cause enough to get his hands dirty and pitch in to help, but she hadn't believed a word of it at the time.

She certainly didn't believe it now. Besides, didn't he have the hots for some other woman? He'd never come to Haffali under such terrible conditions.

Still, she had to know if she was delusional.

"Prince Antony?" she called softly, then clamped a hand over her mouth.

If she *was* imagining things and her staff heard her calling for some prince she'd foolishly kissed in front the whole world, what would they think?

"I am here, as is Pia." Jennifer started as the unexpected reply echoed from somewhere above her. "We will have you out soon," he added.

This time, there was no mistaking Antony's rich voice or his formal manner of speaking. She wasn't delusional, she wasn't imagining him. And he sounded genuinely worried.

"Prince Antony? Pia?" she called out, louder this time.

"Are you all right?" he asked, an edge apparent in his normally commanding tone. "Can you move?"

"I—I think so."

"Stay where you are. I shall be down in a moment."

"No, I'll come to you." She couldn't allow him to risk himself. Besides, how could Antony possibly fit his broad shoulders through such a narrow space? She'd barely made it through herself.

She brushed the grime off her face with the back of her sleeve, then gingerly pushed up to all fours so she could reach the entry. She wondered what had brought Antony back to Haffali, especially after the way they'd left things at the palace. Had he heard about the landslides? Had he really come to help, as Federico suggested Antony would, given the opportunity?

She heard a scuffling noise above her, causing her to look up just in time to catch a faceful of dust as it poofed through the small passage. "You are hurt, Jennifer!," Antony shouted from the opening. "Do not come—"

"Didn't they teach you anything in prince school, Your Highness?" she grumbled, reaching out for the rocks to pull herself toward the exit. "You're not supposed to endanger yourself for some American girl stupid enough to get herself trapped. Your country needs you in one piece."

She managed to get hold of the rocks, and pulled her battered, tired body into the narrow gap. She took a moment to catch her breath, then reached out to propel herself a few feet closer to the hole. Just as she found a handhold, a strong hand reached down and grabbed hers.

"*You* need me, Jennifer."

She craned her neck to look up, and realized he'd somehow managed to move the rocks just enough to maneuver his body inside the opening. He caught hold of her other hand, then gently pulled her the rest of the way through the passage. With help from Pia, he lifted her out into the bright sunlight.

"You all right?" Pia asked, her forehead creased in a deep frown. "You were knocked out for a few minutes there."

"I'm fine, just a wicked headache," Jennifer replied as she stretched her limbs, checking for injuries. Noticing Josef and his mother, she asked, "How did he avoid getting hurt?"

"You landed on him, which meant you took the brunt of the cave-in," Pia explained. "He crawled out from under you and made it out almost by himself."

Jennifer nodded, the image of herself and Josef trying to get out of the hospital coming back to her. "Let's get him to the mess tent. He should be checked out."

"And you, as well," Prince Antony bent down and gently picked her up, then shifted her in his arms so her body rested firmly against his broad chest.

"Put me down," she protested, though her plea sounded half-hearted, even to her own ears. She had to admit, she'd never felt so tired in her life, and she enjoyed the comfort and protection of his powerful arms around her.

"I will not," Antony replied with all the authority of a future king. "You will stay right where you are until a doctor can examine you."

He looked down at her then, and when his gaze locked with hers, she could swear she saw amusement in his eyes.

"What's so funny?" she demanded.

His face broke into a full-fledged grin. "If you must know, this is what they teach us in prince school. Chivalry."

"That's why you came back to Haffali? To be chivalrous?"

"No," his grin changed to a look of seriousness. "I came for you. I was concerned for your safety, and I thought you might need me."

He came for *her?* Just the fact he'd been worried about her made her face warm and her heart race.

It also left her awash in guilt. How could she have thought such terrible things about him? Just because her parents had bad experiences with politicians and socialites, did that automatically mean Prince Antony would act similarly? For the world's hottest tabloid cover boy to say what he just had was as close to an admission of genuine affection as he'd probably ever made. And for him to travel to Rasovo, despite the danger involved for someone in his position, meant he had a strength of character she'd never given him credit for.

Fumbling for an apology, Jennifer began, "I—I'm touched that you thought of me, but I have to tell you—"

"I confess," he added, "I also believe helping the Rasovars is the noble thing for someone in my position to do. I could not turn my back on them."

She swallowed hard. So his trip wasn't really about *her.* "I suppose you were taught how to act nobly in prince school, as well?" she joked, trying to cover her feminine response to being so close to him.

"No. You taught me that." He pulled her closer, leaning his forehead against hers, then brushing his lips against hers for the briefest of moments. "And as you can see, that makes me more than a better prince. It makes me a better man. If we had not met as we did, I would not be here now. And I would not be making the choice I am about to make."

He took her mouth with his possessively, and despite her scrapes and bruises, Jennifer relished his touch. His arms tightened around her protectively as their kiss deepened. Finally, he broke their kiss. "We must get to the mess tent," he whispered, his voice hoarse with desire. "I can't risk having you hurt out here in the open. But we shall resume this later. When everyone is safe once again."

"You've been holding out on me," Pia whispered, her voice filled with accusation. She daubed rubbing alcohol on one of Jennifer's scraped knees, while Jennifer sat on the mess tent table where the doctor had just finished examining her. She shifted on the rough wood, easing her fingers under the ice pack she held against her forehead. She had a feeling the bruise would be a whopper. She replaced the ice pack, then eyed Pia.

"What do you mean?"

"The prince kissed you again. And don't give me that same garbage you did last time about how it was 'nothing.' Prince Antony, ultra-Adonis of the western world, doesn't just fly into the middle of a bombed out camp for nothing!"

Jennifer looked past Pia, making sure Antony was still at the other end of the mess tent talking to Josef's mother, before whispering back, "He only came because he thought it was the noble thing to do."

"Since when? I mean, I know he's big on helping out charities, but according to my cousin, he's a typical royal. A celebrity endorsement here, a little cash there. Not exactly the hands-on type."

Pia stepped back, scrutinized Jennifer's knee a moment, then stuck a gauze bandage over the largest of the cuts. "That should do it." She looked up at Jen-

nifer then, checked the growing bump on her forehead, then in a hushed, serious tone added, "He just
can't stand the thought of you getting hurt any more
than I can. If you ask me, the great playboy thinks
he's fallen in love."

"No way," Jennifer protested. "I work in a refugee camp, for crying out loud. And I'm an American." Her jaw dropped as she thought back to what
he said when he kissed her. "But he...Pia...oh my
gosh—"

"But he what?"

Jennifer set down the ice pack and put a hand to
her now-queasy stomach. "He told me I taught him
how to be noble. That I made him a better man. And
he told me he was about to make an important
choice." She blinked as the realization hit her. "Do
you think he meant—?"

"No!"

"I mean, we haven't known each other that long.
But he makes me so—"

"Stop right there." Pia leaned in close to Jennifer,
making sure no one else in the mess tent could hear
them. "Don't say it. Don't even think it. It would be
the most terrible thing in the world to happen to
you."

Jennifer did a double-take. "Come again?"

"You could never be with him, even if you were
both giddy in love, which I assume you aren't."

"Of course not," Jennifer lied, suddenly defensive.
"But as you say, he's an Adonis. Why would it be
so terrible if I did fall for him?"

"Are you kidding?" Pia hissed. "You'd get your
heart trampled. I mean, there's no way King Eduardo
would stand for his oldest son and heir marrying an

American. He threw a public fit when Prince Antony went out with that Hollywood actress last year, remember?''

"That's true," Jennifer sighed. "Even I heard about that, and I don't read the tabloids."

"Well, from what I remember, the actress said publicly that they weren't really dating, they just went to a couple of movie premieres together or something. But it was still a huge scandal for him to be romantically linked to an American with no aristocratic roots. It didn't help her career, either. The San Riminians thought she was a completely inappropriate match for Antony and threatened to boycott her movies!"

Jennifer hopped off the table and let out a deep breath. "In other words, if I date Antony and Eduardo doesn't like it—"

"Which he certainly won't."

"—then the San Riminians won't support the San Riminian Scholarship Fund, since the recipients come to work here."

Pia spread her arms wide. "Exactly. Keep kissing Antony, and you can kiss the support of the San Riminians goodbye. Plus, just look at how the newspaper portrayed you after Antony kissed you at the palace last week. Believe it or not, gaming halls all over San Rimini are taking bets on whether you'll be the prince's bride. And I hate to tell you what the tabloids say the odds are. Do you really want to live that way?"

Jennifer grazed her fingers through her hair, then rubbed her sore neck.

Try as she might to ignore the fact, she *had* fallen for Antony. Hard.

But as Pia pointed out, the relationship was impossible. Even if by some miracle, he could love her in return, she couldn't risk the future of the refugees over such long odds.

"He'll be back in San Rimini in a few days," Jennifer speculated aloud. "And I'm sure, given the circumstances, he'll forget about me soon enough. I won't encourage him while he's here."

"Smart move." Pia put her hands on her hips, apparently satisfied with Jennifer's response. "Count yourself incredibly lucky he kissed you, and be flattered that he's so attracted to you. But please, please, please, try real hard to keep your heart out of it. You're my best friend, and I don't want to see you hurt."

"I promise," Jennifer replied, though she knew Antony had already made his way into her heart permanently.

Antony stretched his tired legs under Jennifer's battered desk, then took another bite of the chocolate brownie she'd given him. Though it certainly wasn't his usual dining experience, the hard day's work—and the woman who kept him company—convinced him this was the best meal he'd ever eaten.

"This is delicious," Antony commented as he savored another bite of brownie.

Jennifer sat nearby, munching on her own brownie, in the seat Pia usually occupied. For the last fourteen hours, he'd helped as she struggled to put her camp back into operation. The last of the refugees had been located, the mess tent had been turned into a makeshift hospital with what medical equipment they could salvage, a clean water station had been set up, and

the refugees' tents had been put back into habitable
enough shape for a night's rest. They'd accomplished
a lot, but even with everyone working together, they
still hadn't managed to set up a working kitchen. Now
that it was nearly four in the morning, he'd finally
persuaded her to stop for the night so they could get
some food and a few hours' rest. He glanced at the
dark bump on her head for the hundredth time, wondering how she could still function after the day she'd
had.

"You've got to be kidding," she replied between
bites of brownie. "They're just surplus MRE's. I
doubt this is even real chocolate."

Antony raised an eyebrow. "MRE's?"

"Meals Ready to Eat. Military rations donated by
the Rasovar military in case our food supply was ever
contaminated or lost." She laughed, then reached
down into a small cardboard box and retrieved a vac-
uum-packed beige packet she claimed would contain
hash browns once water was added. "Not exactly
haute cuisine, Your Highness. But you're a prince.
Weren't you ever in the military?"

He laughed. Him in the army? "I am afraid not,
though I admit, I often dreamed about it as a boy.
Stories about kings leading their soldiers into battle
fascinated me. If danger ever befell my people, I
would consider it my royal duty to fight to defend
them. But in San Rimini, the crown prince is prohib-
ited from military service. It is considered too great
a risk to my personal safety. So my brothers were
permitted to serve, though I was not."

"But you wanted to?"

"After I learned it was forbidden, I simply did not
think about it. What would be the point?" He stood,

then stretched his arms up to the ceiling of the small trailer that served as the camp's headquarters.

"Yet you came here," Jennifer observed. "That's a risk to your personal safety."

"Yes. And like military service, it was forbidden to me. My father will be furious when he discovers what I've done."

All his life he'd done his duty without giving his personal desires a second thought. Yet at this moment, his personal desire for Jennifer filled his soul, made him want to crush her to him and never release her. And for once, letting his desires rule his actions didn't seem like such a bad idea. Coming here to help would make him a better prince.

And, no matter what the cost, he knew making her his bride would make him a better man.

He stopped stretching, then took a seat across from Jennifer, hoping to capture her undivided attention.

"When you came to the palace, you told me that everyone has choices in life. It is a common saying in my country. However, until you said it, I never considered that it could apply to me."

He reached forward, cupping her chin in his hand and allowing his thumb to run across her smooth, soft skin. Her face turned serious, and he knew she was listening carefully.

Diving in, he began, "Kissing you in the palace was the first real choice I ever made that was not dictated to me at birth. Every cause I have supported, every school I have attended, and every single woman I have dated were thoroughly analyzed and approved by my parents ahead of time. I didn't want to do these things, but—except in the case of dating—I rarely argued. And even in those rare instances when I made my opinion known, my parents got their way. Even now, my father is working to arrange my marriage to Lady Francesca Benedetta, since, in his view, I have failed to find an acceptable bride.''

Jennifer's face became unreadable to him as he moved his hand along her cheek, then ran his fingers into her lush red curls. How many days and nights had he dreamed of her hair since they'd met? ''I can never thank you enough, Jennifer, for making me see that I *do* have choices in life. I know that kiss probably angered you, especially after the horrible way the press covered it. I might have even cost you and your organization credibility.''

''Apology accepted,'' she mumbled, turning her face away.

He shook his head, and gently caressed her cheek, forcing her to look him in the eye. ''I didn't say *I* was sorry. Despite the fact that the press caught us, I cannot bring myself to regret that kiss. If I had not kissed you, had not taken the time to consider that perhaps I do have choices in my life, I would never have come here to Rasovo. I would not have saved Josef, and I would not have saved you. And most important, I would not know the satisfaction of helping others in the way you do. I cannot thank you enough for that.''

Jennifer stood, forcing him to drop his hand from her soft face and putting a distance between them he didn't want. ''You're welcome, Your Highness. If it makes you a better prince, I'm honored to have helped in some small way.''

''Some small way? Do you not realize—''

She stepped past him to the trailer window, cutting him off midsentence. ''I do realize. More than you know. But the sun's coming up. We won't get any sleep at all if we don't try to grab a catnap now." She made her way to the trailer door and popped it open. As she looked at him, her face showed no emotion. Nothing to indicate that she'd heard or understood what he was trying to tell her. "Why don't I show you where you can rest undisturbed?"

Antony stood, stunned. What had just transpired? He'd been ready to confess his love for her, trying to tell her all she'd meant to him, then she'd suddenly gone cold. Had he misjudged her? Put too much stock into the sweet kisses they shared as he carried her from the hospital wreckage? Misconstrued their stolen glances as they'd mended tents and organized the mess area? He'd never professed love to a woman before—it was too risky for a man in his position— so perhaps he'd gone about it the wrong way.

He strode to the door, then allowed his body to brush against hers as he stepped out into the early dawn.

No reaction from Jennifer whatsoever. *Damn.* His stomach dropped as if he'd just been told the palace burned down.

Schooling his features and checking his posture as if about to greet dignitaries at a state dinner, he nodded that she should lead the way. He'd never been rejected by a woman before, and pride wouldn't allow him to show how deeply it affected him.

She looked at him for a moment, and her eyes filled for the briefest of moments with pain and longing. But the second he registered the hurt on her face it disappeared, replaced by the confidence of a relief worker with a job to do. She scooted ahead of him. "This way, Your Highness."

So he *had* said something wrong. She had fallen in love with him, too. He was certain of it. But what could he say to make her realize the depth of his feelings for her?

"Jennifer. Please stop. I must break the air between us." He reached for her arm and spun her around to face him. A grin of amusement lit up her face, but he certainly didn't find the situation funny.

"Jennifer?"

"I believe you mean *clear* the air, Your Highness. One can break wind—which has an entirely different meaning—or one can clear the air."

"What does break wind—"

"Please, you don't want to know." Her smile widened and she shook her head, dismissing the subject. "Let's just say it's not a phrase a prince would use."

He frowned. He would press her for the meaning later. "Then I wish to clear the air. If that is what it means to discuss what has happened between us. And what I wish to happen."

The smile left her face. "Your Highness, given the circumstances...I mean, Lady Francesca...I can't see what we need to discuss."

So that was his mistake. "This has nothing to do with Lady Francesca. It has everything to do with us."

"Really, there's no need to explain. Someone in your position must—"

"Must learn to make choices, smart choices that will benefit not only my people, but will benefit me as well. And you, Jennifer Allen, benefit me."

"I—"

Before she could argue, he grabbed her shoulders. He couldn't allow himself to lose her now. "*You* are my choice. You, Jennifer. Not Francesca or Bianca or any of the other women my father has forced me to date. And it is my most sincere hope that I will be yours."

He eased her closer, then wrapped her in his arms so she couldn't escape again. "You taught me to make choices for *me*. How can you now tell me that I must choose Francesca when it is you I want to hold, you I want to kiss, you I want to be with?"

She shook her head, but didn't pull away. Knowing he could express himself even more eloquently with his body than in his error-prone English, he crushed his mouth to hers, striving to convince her that Lady Francesca was the furthest thing from his mind.

She hesitated at his touch, but then a shiver ran through her body, and she leaned into him, snaking her arms around his waist and returning his kiss with gusto.

He thought his body would burst from pent-up desire as she allowed him to taste her, embrace her, possess her.

This was the Jennifer he wanted. Passionate about her cause, passionate about the people she cared for, and—most of all—passionate about him. As their kiss deepened, he couldn't help but realize that no woman had ever kissed him as Jennifer did now, with no ulterior motive, no desire to make him believe she was something she wasn't.

Jennifer was kissing him because she wanted to kiss *him*, not because she wanted to ensnare a wealthy prince.

He fell to his knees in the dirt, pulling Jennifer with him, his mouth never leaving hers, so strong was his hunger for her. He reveled in her clean, just-soap scent, then inhaled sharply as her hands made their way from his waist down to tentatively cup his rear, pulling his lower body tight against hers. A jolt of sweet fire pounded through his spinal cord at the sensation, bringing him to a full, hot state of arousal.

Damn if he didn't want to make love to her right there in the dusty road. His heart thudded in his ears as she nuzzled against him, kissing him as no woman should ever kiss a proper prince.

"Antony—"

How many nights had he dreamed of hearing her call him by his given name, rather than "Your Highness?" Fantasized about melding her body to his?

He allowed his lips to wander down to her neck, savoring the taste of her sweet, freckled skin. Her breath echoed in his ear, her heart pounded against his. For the first time in his life, he knew with absolute certainty that he'd found the woman meant to be his bride. A woman who could love him as a prince and as a man.

"Do you have any idea how much I love you?" he heard himself say as he kissed the base of her throat. And he knew with all his heart that he meant it.

"Antony. Antony," she stammered, her breath catching. "We have to stop."

"No one is watching," he whispered against her neck, then kissed and sucked his way back up to her ear. "The sun is hardly up."

"It's not..." she ran her hands up his back, then around to hold his face, forcing his gaze to lock with hers. "I don't want to stop. But we have to."

Then he heard it. A low thump-thump-thump he'd believed only a moment ago to be his thundering heartbeat. Now, listening more carefully, he recognized the persistent thrum as the sound of his royal helicopter. He should have known Guilio would return at the crack of dawn to bring more supplies and check on his well-being.

He closed his eyes for a moment and leaned his forehead against hers, savoring the caress of her fingertips against his cheeks. He let out a deep breath, then met her gaze once more. "You are right. We have to. But if you do not want to—"

"Antony!"

"Then we shall simply resume later." He gave Jennifer a quick, parting kiss, then leapt to his feet, offering her a hand. He couldn't help but grin, realizing what a dirty, disheveled pair they made. Jennifer's shirt rested askew on her shoulders, her hair looked as if she hadn't brushed it for a week. He loved that he'd made her look like that.

"I suppose work should come first," Jennifer commented as she brushed the dirt off her shorts and adjusted her shirt. She met his gaze and laughed, "Though *you* hardly look like you're ready for the kind of work you usually do."

"No?"

"No. Most definitely not." She pointed to his pants, and when he followed her line of sight, he saw his usually clean khakis now sported mud on the knees.

"Well. I shall have to speak to my valet about this." He gestured to the helicopter. "We should hurry if we are to meet Guilio."

Jennifer nodded, then started up the hill toward the helicopter, now circling the helipad. He followed, half-admiring Jennifer from behind, half-worried about what the return of the royal helicopter really meant—an all-too-soon return to his royal life. With any luck, he'd come up with a way to explain himself to his father before he and Guilio made it back to San Rimini.

Antony took Jennifer's elbow to help her step up a sharp rise in the hill, then looked up to see the helicopter touch down and its whirring blades begin to slow. Letting go of Jennifer, he waved to Guilio, then realized the helicopter had two occupants. There was no mistaking the proud figure occupying the seat beside his pilot. He stopped walking for a moment.

Jennifer turned to look at him. "What's wrong?"

He forced a smile to his face. "Nothing. Let's go."

Chapter Ten

Jennifer let out a deep breath, then licked her lips as she and the prince climbed the last hundred feet to reach the helipad.

The helicopter's cargo would be a boon to the camp until the Red Cross arrived with more supplies, but Jennifer found it hard to concentrate on her job.

Her mind had followed her body—firmly wrapping itself around Antony.

Hadn't Pia warned her that if she kissed him again, her heart could be lost? Well, now she'd done it—kissed him as she'd kissed no other man in her life—and Pia had been right. Even now, her heart beat faster than the helicopter blades and her cheeks felt as if she'd been under the hot Rasovo sun for hours, though it was only daybreak.

Antony had felt it too—the nervousness, the anticipation, the heart-stopping attraction—of that she was certain. But when he'd seen the royal helicopter, he'd stiffened. Sure, he'd acted as if it didn't matter and continued to romance her, but something inside him changed when the helicopter invaded their privacy. Then he'd hesitated when they were only halfway up the hill, as if preparing to turn back into his oh-so-formal self. And as Pia predicted, reminding her that she could never be a part of his upper-crust world. Even if she had begun to think of him as *Antony* instead of *Prince Antony*.

Jennifer kicked a rock out of the way and glanced up at the helicopter again. Soon Antony would be flying back to San Rimini with her heart in tow. He'd realize that it was best for all involved if he returned to his duties, married Lady Francesca as his father wished, and became a solid, reliable king to his people.

And she'd be pursuing her own duties here in Rasovo, trying to forget him by focusing her attention on the people who mattered most to her. Or, at least, on the people who *should* matter most. After all, a relationship with him could hurt the Rasovars, if the people of San Rimini viewed her as they had that American actress.

It was the way of the world, wasn't it? The way things were supposed to be. He had his duties, she had hers. If those duties conflicted with a potential relationship, then the relationship had to go. The well-being of hundreds—or in Antony's case, hundreds of thousands—of people depended on them doing their jobs.

Stepping from the rocky hill onto the helipad, she flinched in surprise as Antony reached up to cup her elbow again, his firm, warm grip ensuring she didn't trip. He didn't look directly at her, instead releasing her elbow and striding one step ahead of her to the helicopter.

She squared her shoulders and put on her best face. No, even knowing that Antony would soon leave, she couldn't bring herself to regret kissing him. For the rest of her life, she'd be able to tuck their time together away in her heart, dreaming of what could have been if their relationship had moved beyond more than stolen kisses. She'd never have believed it of a prince, but Antony cared. His heart drove him to overcome the barriers of his position and find ways to personally give of himself to those in need, so much so that he was willing to risk his safety.

And she had grown as well. Getting to know Antony—learning that his concern for his subjects and for those in need were what truly motivated him in life, rather than a desire for political gain or popularity in the press—made her realize that she'd misjudged those in power all her life. Those preconceptions had probably stopped her from connecting with those who genuinely cared about the Rasovars and were in a position to help them more than once, and she hadn't even realized it. From now on, Antony in her life or not, she knew she'd be better at her own job for having met him.

In the meantime, there was no way she'd let Antony see her heartbreak. Or Guilio, for that matter. She'd get her job done and enjoy what little time she and Antony had left, even if that time was spent under the watchful eyes of Antony's pilot and her assistant camp director.

"Jennifer?" Antony's deep, rich voice pierced her thoughts, making her stomach flip as always with his heavily accented pronunciation of her name.

"Yes?"

"You might have noticed that my pilot is not alone."

No, she hadn't. But as the door to the helicopter opened and Guilio stepped out, her heart caught in her throat. There could be no mistaking the serene figure remaining inside.

"The king?"

No wonder he'd suddenly turned formal. And so much for relishing any time she and Antony had left.

"Should I leave you two alone? Maybe—"

"No."

She clamped her mouth shut as Guilio assisted the king out of the helicopter. Even from her position behind Antony, she could tell by the king's drawn brows and set mouth that he wasn't happy to be at Haffali. At all.

"Come with me." She blinked at Antony's suggestion, but followed him across the last few steps to where his father was waiting.

"Prince Antony." The king's expression grew even darker as he uttered his son's name.

"Your Highness." Antony's tone gave no indication that he knew of his father's displeasure. "I'd like you to meet Ms. Jennifer Allen. Since you weren't able to make it to the San Riminian Scholarship Fund dinner, you missed meeting her." He turned and smiled at Jennifer, and she instantly recognized how hard he was working to smooth the waters with his father. "As you know, Father, Ms. Allen's speech at the dinner was instrumental in raising a great amount of money to support San Rimini's college students."

"Ms. Allen. A pleasure to meet you."

As Jennifer shook his hand, she sensed a calm,

well-controlled interior lurked beneath his stern expression. His thin-rimmed glasses, rich charcoal suit, cream-colored shirt and expensive tie lent him the same air of confidence she'd noticed in Antony when they'd met. His hair was graying, though it hadn't thinned as in most middle-aged men, and the crinkles around his eyes made him appear even more distinguished.

She imagined that in twenty or so years, Antony would look very much like his father.

"I'm honored to meet you as well, Your Highness," Jennifer managed. "Prince Antony has done a great deal for the Rasovars. We're so pleased that he was able to personally bring supplies during our crisis—and that you are doing the same. You have no idea what a morale boost this will be for the refugees. Thank you."

The king raised his hand. "I am afraid you misunderstand, Ms. Allen. I am glad you appreciate all my son has done here, but unfortunately we cannot stay. He has a pressing engagement, so to speak, tonight at the palace. After we have unloaded these supplies, we must return to San Rimini."

"I'm so sorry to hear that." Jennifer forced herself to keep her chin high despite the monarch's brush-off. Antony might look scruffy now, and she might finally feel comfortable around him, despite the fact that he was a famous royal, but the king's stately presence reminded her that she wasn't in his league.

Not that she needed reminding.

Antony put a hand on his father's back, gently urging him forward. "You look tired from the flight, Father. Perhaps a brief trip to the mess tent for some coffee would be in order? It will take some time to unload the supplies, so you might as well see some of the camp, then rest a while."

The king frowned. "I suppose."

"Of course you shall join us, Jennifer?" Antony shot her a look that said it wasn't an invitation. He expected her to come. Why, after his father's polite-but-firm attempts to yank his son away from her, she couldn't fathom. By encouraging her to join them, and keeping his father's questions at bay, he was probably digging himself an even deeper hole.

"Jennifer?"

"Of course. I'll find a couple of people to unload the helicopter in the meantime."

Fifteen minutes later, having finally reached the mess tent, Jennifer had shown King Eduardo as much of the camp as she suspected he wanted to see. Probably more. He didn't seem to object to Antony's support of the Rasovo Relief Society in general, but from his gruff responses as they walked through the camp, it was obvious the king wished his son was a little less involved.

Probably because of Antony's "pressing engagement," which she imagined had something to do with Lady Francesca.

She reached onto a small shelf in the rear of the mess tent, grabbing the least battered cup she could find to fill with coffee for the king. Even as she did so, she felt the old man's gaze fixed on her, studying her. She wondered if he'd noticed the same dirt and grass stains on her clothing as on Antony's. If so, it was no wonder he didn't seem to warm to her.

It was his top priority to put his son on the throne with a suitable queen at his side. A rough-around-the-edges American who dug latrines and set up tents for a living didn't fit the bill. And the fact that Antony had flown into dangerous territory to assist her didn't help matters.

She filled the cup from a large urn, then returned to the long wooden table where the king sat across from Antony, who'd already helped himself to a cup of water.

"I apologize for the quality of the coffee, Your Highness." She reached across the table, setting the tin cup in front of the stoic king. "And I'm afraid we're out of bone china at the moment. This is the best we have."

"I am sure it will be fine." Ignoring her for the moment, he turned to Antony. "Son, how long do you believe it will take to unload the supplies? We have some urgent business we should discuss."

Antony quirked an eyebrow at Jennifer.

"Half an hour, Your Highness," she answered, suddenly feeling like an intruder. "Would you like me to run back to the helipad to check on their progress?"

"Thank you, Ms. Allen. That would be appreciated."

"No, Jennifer." Antony stood, his mouth set in a tight line. "I would rather you stay."

The king's forehead creased. He shot a warning look at Antony, then reached into the inside pocket of his suit jacket and pulled out something small and black. "I am afraid this is official royal business, Ms. Allen. You will let us know when Guilio is ready to make the flight back to San Rimini?"

Jennifer nodded to the king, then started to back out of the tent. It wasn't any pending matter of state—she wasn't that obtuse—but no way would she put herself in the middle of an argument between father and son. Especially this father and son.

"Jennifer, *stay.*" Antony's voice exuded an authority Jennifer thought reserved for those already on the throne. "This may be official royal business, but it directly concerns you."

"I really don't think—"

The king's face darkened. "*Fine,* Antony. Perhaps she should stay. It will benefit her to hear this firsthand." He stood and turned toward Jennifer, then wagged a finger at her as if he were eighty and she were a two-year-old. "However, I trust that you will not go running to the tabloids with word of this discussion. It is to stay in this tent. Is that clear?"

Jennifer strode toward the table, suddenly enraged that the king would think such a thing. "After the way the tabloids treated me last week? Just what kind of person do you think I am, Your Highness?"

The king's eyes widened a fraction, and she schooled herself to keep her anger in check. "I apologize, Your Highness. If Antony insists, I'll stay. But you must understand I have no desire to be here while you two argue, let alone go spreading your discussion to tabloid reporters. I would never, *never,* speak to them about your family. I have far too much respect for Antony—and too little for those stupid rags—to speak to them."

King Eduardo tilted his head, as if accepting her explanation, then gestured to the empty area of the bench next to Antony. Jennifer studied them both for a minute, decided that she'd made her point, then took the seat next to Antony.

"What you do not know, Ms. Allen, is that due to health concerns, I may not be on the throne much longer. For that reason, it is imperative my son marry a suitable bride in the very near future. I have tried, without success, to introduce him to appropriate women.''

"Which only succeeded in giving me a playboy reputation," Antony muttered under his breath, just loud enough for Jennifer to hear.

The king either didn't hear or ignored the comment. "Due to time constraints, I have asked my son to select a bride by year's end. This is why having that tabloid reporter snap photographs of you kissing at the dinner was so unfortunate. It made him appear unready for marriage, which is why I had a few palace insiders tip the reporter to the fact that Antony was an unwilling participant.''

"You what?" Antony and Jennifer cried simultaneously.

He held up a hand. "I realize that it was neither accurate, nor flattering to you, Ms. Allen, and I apologize. However, I had to protect my family. I was deep in negotiations with Countess Benedetta, arranging a marriage between Antony and her daughter, Lady Francesca. I could not allow those discussions to falter.''

Jennifer balled her hands into fists under the table. "You not only made me look like, like a *hussy,* Your Highness, but you may have seriously impaired my ability to find workers from San Rimini.''

"I know. And again, I apologize. Once this mess is cleared up, I will personally encourage San Riminians to support Antony's scholarship fund, as well as the Rasovo Relief Society. Which is why I needed to come here to locate my son.''

He pushed the small black item that he'd taken

from his pocket earlier toward Antony. Though she'd never owned a velvet box in her life, she knew the moment she saw it that it held a ring. And that ring wasn't meant for her.

Antony slowly opened the box to reveal a delicate, jewel-encrusted gold band. "Mother's ring," he murmured.

"She was proud to wear it." As Eduardo looked at the ring, Jennifer thought she heard a wistfulness creep into his voice. "And I wish she was alive to wear it now. But you knew it would always come to you, to give to your bride."

He cleared his throat, and his voice became strong and sure once more. "Tonight, Lady Francesca and her mother will be at the palace for dinner. You will present her this ring, and ask her to be your bride. It has all been arranged."

He glanced at Jennifer. "I am sorry, Ms. Allen. I know you are an honorable woman, and I believe you have strong feelings for my son. But Lady Francesca has shown herself to be an appropriate bride for my son, and my country needs a queen and heir if Prince Antony is to take the throne. It is the way it must be."

Jennifer nodded to the king. Her insides clenched, and she felt sure her heart would break, but she knew King Eduardo wasn't telling her anything she didn't already know, deep down inside.

The door to the tent breezed open, startling the three. Pia stood in the doorway, stunned when she saw the king. "Oh. Your Highness." She curtseyed, though Jennifer had to admit it looked strange, since Pia was in her work clothes. "I hope I'm not interrupting. Prince Antony's pilot wanted me to let him know that the helicopter is ready.''

''Thank you,'' the king replied. Pia glanced at Jennifer, and her eyes widened as if to say, *what the heck is going on?* before she ducked back out the door.

''I promise, Ms. Allen, once the ceremony has taken place, I will do my best to make this up to you. I shall make certain Antony continues the San Riminian Scholarship Fund to send our students to work here, and I will personally encourage my friends to support it.''

He stood, smoothed his charcoal suit, then nodded to Antony. ''Shall we? We only have a few hours before Countess Benedetta and her daughter arrive at the palace, and there are preparations to be made.''

''Not yet.'' Without standing, Antony snapped the ring box shut, then rolled it over in his hands. He looked up at his father, and Jennifer saw his Adam's apple bob in a hard swallow.

''Excuse me?''

''I have followed your wishes all my life. But for once—just this one time—I ask that you listen to my opinion first. I know that it is my duty to marry a fit bride, and that Francesca does meet the criteria for becoming a diTalora queen. And I understand your urgency to have me marry—you yourself married at nineteen when your father showed signs of his illness, and it was the best thing for our country at the time. However, I believe I have a better solution to the problem.''

The king shook his head. ''There is no other solution. You *must* marry.''

Antony continued, undaunted. ''That is not true.

You have stated that you would allow Federico to take the throne if I do not marry.''

"Son—"

"Please, let me finish. Do it as a favor to Jennifer, if nothing else. I believe you owe her that much after what you told the tabloids.''

"Ms. Allen has nothing to do with this.''

Jennifer looked at Antony, silently begging him not to continue. What good would it do, besides let her down even harder? "Antony, it's all right. Marry Francesca. It's what's best for your country. And in the end, what's best for your country will make you happy.''

Antony smiled, then reached out to touch her cheek. "I know. Which is why I wish to marry you.''

Chapter Eleven

Jennifer's mouth dropped open. Had Antony just said he wanted to *marry* her? How could that be possible?

He couldn't marry her. No matter how much he might think he loved her, no matter how determined he was to ditch Lady Francesca. His father, not to mention his subjects, would reject the idea outright. Antony even said that if he didn't marry Francesca, he'd lose the throne to Federico!

No. It just wasn't possible. Even if by some chance, they *did* marry, the hatred the San Riminians would feel for her would deeply affect the Rasovars. She'd have no hope of finding enough workers to sustain camp operations. As much as she loved Antony, as much as she dreamed of spending the rest of her life with him, she couldn't harm the people she'd come to know, love—and most importantly, protect—here in Rasovo.

"Prince Antony!" King Eduardo's face went blood-red. "You forget yourself!"

Antony exploded out of his seat. "Please, Father. Hear me out. I believe Jennifer would be a much better choice than Francesca, both for my personal well-being and for the future of San Rimini."

"Antony," she put a hand on his arm. "We could never be married. It wouldn't work."

He looked down at her, his intense gaze holding her motionless. She couldn't help but notice how regal and commanding he looked, despite his soiled clothing and less-than civilized surroundings. "Do you love me, Jennifer?"

She swallowed. "Yes."

A smile leapt to Antony's face.

"But…"

"Then you must hear me out, as well."

He grabbed the velvet box from the table. "What do you know of this ring, Father? Of its history?"

The king crossed his arms over his chest and shrugged, apparently reconciling himself to the fact that he would have to listen to his son if he ever wanted to get on the helicopter. "It has been in our family for generations. Nearly every diTalora queen has worn it as a symbol of her love for our country."

"And why has it symbolized love?"

"Do you have a point?"

Antony turned to face Jennifer. "About five hundred years ago, our great Queen Danae purchased diamonds and rubies from foreign traders, then had them crafted into a ring. Because such stones were rare at the time, the ring was considered priceless, and it became her favorite possession. Many San Riminians secretly disliked her, because she'd been born Greek and they felt she married into the diTalora family to gain wealth, not because she felt any loyalty to the diTaloras or to our country.''

He opened the box and withdrew the thin gold band, running his thumb over the tiny jewels which surrounded it. "When a famine struck the country, Queen Danae immediately traded the ring to a Rasovar prince for foodstuffs. Though she was a foreigner, she loved the people of San Rimini so much she offered up her precious ring to feed them. For her selfless actions, she is now remembered fondly by the people. Her son purchased the ring back from Rasovo after her death and presented it to his bride, stating that no other symbol could better represent the love the diTalora family had for each other, or for the people who allowed them to rule. It has been worn by every diTalora queen since then."

He held up the ring and stared down his father. "It is my firm belief that a diTalora queen should possess the same qualities as Queen Danae before she may wear this ring. She should be selfless, putting the well-being of others before her own dreams of wealth or privilege. None of the women you have chosen for me to date, Lady Francesca included, meet these criteria. True, they have the proper bloodline to be queen, but, as you might recall, Queen Danae did not come from a titled family. She merely possessed the spirit of a queen. Yet she is the queen our country most reveres."

"Son," the king shook his head. "I agree that a queen must be selfless. But these are different times. The people of San Rimini demand a queen with aristocratic blood."

"And so they did in Queen Danae's time." He turned to Jennifer, and she could swear she saw the beginnings of tears in his eyes. "Jennifer, I love you as I have loved no other woman. You have seen me the way I've longed to be seen, for the person I am, rather than for the person the tabloids picture me to be." He paused for a moment, as if struggling to find the words in English. "You also have shown me what it means to care for people. And how I can better care for them. That makes me a better prince, but more importantly, it makes me a better man. I have never felt as—as *filled* inside—as I have these past few weeks with you. Even if it means I shall never take the throne, I want to marry you. I would be empty without you." He pressed the ring into her hand and held it there. "Jennifer, would you be my wife?"

"Antony..." she stared at their hands, feeling the ring clamped between them, knowing the enormity of what Antony asked. How could she possibly respond?

"Ms. Allen," the king's voice cut into her. "You would marry my son, even if it meant he would forfeit the throne?"

"No." She gulped and squeezed Antony's hand. "I mean, I would. But I can't ask that of him."

Hot tears burned her cheeks as she looked at Antony. Fighting to keep her composure, she explained, "The people of San Rimini love you. They want you to be their next king. Not Federico or anyone else. And I know you'll make a wonderful king. I can't..." she tried not to sniffle, but did anyway. "I can't stand in the way of that. Besides," she shook her head at the king, "I know that when Antony dated that American actress, your subjects were upset. They would think even worse of me. And even though I could handle that, I wouldn't want Antony to suffer for it. And I wouldn't want the people of this camp to suffer.

In the end they would be hurt the most, because San Riminians would stop supporting the scholarship fund.''

She bit her lip, knowing she was throwing happiness away, but also knowing that it had to be done, for so many reasons. ''I'm so sorry, Antony. But just as your people rely on you to fulfill a certain role and be their king, the people of this camp rely on me to do what's in their best interest. I promised them that, and my duty to them is no less important than yours to your people.'' Taking a deep breath, she released Antony's hand, leaving the tiny ring in his open palm. ''As much as I love you, I can't marry you.''

Unable to look Antony in the eye, Jennifer stood and ran for the door of the tent.

Antony dropped to the bench, his chest pounding and head spinning as if he'd just survived a hundred-foot drop off a cliff.

Jennifer said no.

Now he'd lost everything. His father's respect, Jennifer's love and the throne. He couldn't bear to rule without her. And now that he knew her, knew what it really was to have a woman respect him for himself and treat him as an equal, he couldn't stand the thought of marrying another.

As Jennifer yanked open the thin wooden door to the mess tent, he struggled to find the words that would bring her back.

He couldn't just let her go, could he?

''Ms. Allen!''

Both he and Jennifer stopped and stared at the king. Antony had almost forgotten his father's presence, he'd been so overcome with feeling for Jennifer. And what he was about to lose.

"Yo-your Highness?"

"Come back to the table. I have not excused you."

Jennifer's chin jutted out. "Forgive me, but I am not one of your subjects."

"That, young lady, is what I wish to discuss. Please, sit."

Jennifer stared at his father for a second, and Antony sensed an almost palpable change in his father's demeanor. "Please, Jennifer?" he asked.

Her hand gripped the door handle, then she slowly let it go, turned, and approached the table. Without sitting, she eyed the king. "I'm listening."

King Eduardo cleared his throat. "The reason the people of San Rimini did not approve of the American actress was because *I* did not approve of her. She cared nothing for San Rimini, only for what it could give her career to be seen with my son. It had nothing to do with the fact she was American."

He ran a shaky hand through his thick hair. "Though I would prefer my son to marry someone from San Rimini, with a natural love of our country, you have clearly demonstrated your concern for our people by asking Antony to marry Francesca, if that is what the people want. And you have demonstrated a selflessness I only knew in my own late wife, Aletta, by giving so much of yourself to the Rasovars."

Antony stood, not believing his father's words. "What are you saying?"

"I'm saying that if Jennifer wants to marry you, I will not stand in the way any longer. Nor will I make you relinquish the throne to your brother. Jennifer would make a far better queen than Lucrezia, in any event." The king turned to Jennifer, placing a hand on her shoulder. "I apologize for any pain I have caused you, my dear, but you must understand, I may not survive my illness and have to ensure my people have the best possible queen on the throne. I admit, in my heart, I had hoped Antony would marry someone of royal blood. But now I see that he would never be happy, no matter how much I encourage him. He would be happiest with you, and I believe you will help him become an even better role model for our people."

"Thank you, Your Highness." Jennifer brushed a streaky tear from her cheek with the back of her hand. "Still—"

"I will do what I can to support the Rasovars. If I support the scholarship fund and speak highly of your efforts with this camp, my friends will, as well. What happened with that actress will not happen with you. Please, do not worry." With that, he dropped his hand and headed for the door of the tent. "Now, I must return to San Rimini. Countess Benedetta will arrive soon, and I must find a delicate way to handle this. Will you be joining me, Antony?"

Antony studied Jennifer, unable to read her emotions through her tear-filled eyes. "Give me a minute."

The king nodded. "I shall be with Guilio."

The second the door swung shut behind his father, Antony bolted over the table and pulled Jennifer into his arms. "I am so sorry, Jennifer. I did not realize my father would...I'd hoped to ask you before he came, get our feelings out before—"

"Shh. It's okay." She buried her face in his shoulder. Her hot tears wet through the fabric of his shirt, and she shuddered in his embrace before wrapping her arms around him. Unable to express the tumult in his heart, he could only whisper, *"Per favore?"*

She leaned back from his embrace. "What?"

"Please. It means please."

She blinked, confused. "I know what it means. Please *what?*"

"Please, Jennifer, would you marry me?"

She couldn't help but grin, and reached up to place her hand against his cheek. "Only if you promise me one thing."

"Anything."

"Don't try to improve your English. I always want you to call me *'Zhennifer.'*"

"No," he whispered. *"Princess* Jennifer." He pulled her to him, covering her mouth with hot kisses full of promise.

Epilogue

Nine months later

"**W**here in the world have you been?" Jennifer blinked up at Antony, taking in his jogging pants and fleece vest as he stood beside their bed in the early morning light, his face flushed. She glanced at the tall bedroom window, partially covered by heavy velvet curtains. The sun had just appeared over the horizon, casting the palace gardens in a warm glow. "It's not even 7:00 a.m.!"

"And we weren't in bed until after midnight," Antony flashed her a devilish grin. "But our wedding was so wonderful, so magical, I couldn't help but feel energized this morning. I joined my father on his morning run through the park."

Jennifer pushed herself up in bed, still trying to get used to the fact that she had spent her first night in Antony's room. And still reeling from the exhilaration of it all.

"I'm so glad he's feeling better," she smiled. "And that he's back to running again. He missed it so much. But that's no excuse for you to leave me on our wedding night."

He pulled off the fleece vest, kicked off his running shoes, then sat down on the bed beside her, his face full of mischief. "What should I do to make it up to you?"

Jennifer looked him over. "I can think of a lot of possibilities."

"I bet." He reached over to her night table and grabbed the morning paper. "I picked this up while I was out. You can guess what is covered on the front page." He leaned over and kissed her, slowly and tenderly, then handed her the paper. "Why don't you read it while I take a shower?"

She rolled the paper up and swatted him with it. How had she ever lived life without him? she wondered. He made her head spin and her heart pound just by being in the same room, let alone by kissing her.

As he stood, he added, "When you are finished, perhaps you can join me? After all, this is our honeymoon."

She unrolled the paper and winked as he strode to his private bath. "I'd better read fast, I suppose."

"*Per favore,*" he laughed over his shoulder. "I had Federico call one of the gaming halls to place a bet for me yesterday."

"What?"

"You shall see," he gestured to the paper before disappearing into the bath.

Jennifer looked down at the paper, and couldn't help but sigh when she saw the picture on the front page. Her, wrapped in Antony's arms, sharing a passionate kiss on the balcony of the royal palace. And this time, they hadn't cared who snapped their picture.

She brushed a tear from her cheek, then read the article.

Prince Charming Weds His Cinderella
San Riminians Rejoice
as Prince Antony Finally Marries

THE ROYAL PALACE, SAN RIMINI (AP)—In the tradition of Prince Edward and Sophie Rhys-Jones of Great Britain, Crown Prince Antony Lorenzo diTalora today wed a working girl, Ms. Jennifer Allen of the United States, at the San Rimini Royal Palace.

The simplicity of the couple's nuptials stunned many, given Prince Antony's position as first in line to one of the longest-held thrones in all Europe. The guest list was limited to two hundred carefully selected individuals, including members of the diTalora and Allen families, several representatives of San Rimini's parliament, and a group from the Haffali refugee camp in Rasovo, where the former Ms. Allen worked as camp director. Members of several European royal families also attended the celebration.

The blushing bride looked absolutely smashing in a white silk gown designed especially for her by Kovat of Rasovo—a gift given by the fashionable design house after the bride cared for the owner's young son, Josef Kovat, at the Haffali camp last year.

The newlyweds will honeymoon later this

week in an undisclosed location. Afterward, the bride has pledged to continue working for the Rasovo Relief Society in their efforts to rebuild Rasovo after its recent civil war. She plans to host several spots on a local educational station about the history of Rasovo, and will be sponsoring two recruiting events for the organization early next month. Prince Antony tells the San Riminian National News he supports his wife's decision to stay involved in the organization "in every way." He himself has expanded his San Riminian Scholarship Fund, recently announcing plans to host at least six fundraising events for the program in the coming months.

As for heirs to the throne? Both the prince and the new princess have confided to friends that they can't wait to have children.

Gaming halls throughout San Rimini have already started taking bets on a birth date.

Jennifer set the paper aside, shaking her head. Springing from the bed, she yelled, "You already placed a bet?!"

Antony poked his head around the door just in time to catch Jennifer in his arms. She laughed, then reached up to lace her fingers through his hair and pull his flushed face down to hers. "Well, then," she whispered. "I'll have to help you win it."

* * * * *

CALL THE ONES YOU LOVE OVER THE HOLIDAYS!

Save $25 off future book purchases when you buy any four Harlequin® or Silhouette® books in October, November and December 2001,

PLUS

receive a phone card good for 15 minutes of long-distance calls to anyone you want in North America!

WHAT AN INCREDIBLE DEAL!

Just fill out this form and attach 4 proofs of purchase (cash register receipts) from October, November and December 2001 books, and Harlequin Books will send you a coupon booklet worth a total savings of $25 off future purchases of Harlequin® and Silhouette® books, AND a 15-minute phone card to call the ones you love, anywhere in North America.

Please send this form, along with your cash register receipts as proofs of purchase, to:
In the USA: Harlequin Books, P.O. Box 9057, Buffalo, NY 14269-9057
In Canada: Harlequin Books, P.O. Box 622, Fort Erie, Ontario L2A 5X3
Cash register receipts must be dated no later than December 31, 2001.
Limit of 1 coupon booklet and phone card per household.
Please allow 4-6 weeks for delivery.

I accept your offer! Enclosed are 4 proofs of purchase. Please send me my coupon booklet and a 15-minute phone card:

Name: _____

Address: _____ City: _____

State/Prov.: _____ Zip/Postal Code: _____

Account Number (if available): _____

---

097 KJB DAGL
PHQ4013

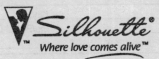

Silhouette®

INTIMATE MOMENTS™
is proud to present

Romancing the Crown

With the help of their powerful allies, the royal family of Montebello is determined to find their missing heir. But the search for the beloved prince is not without danger—or passion!

This exciting twelve-book series begins in January and continues throughout the year with these fabulous titles:

Available at your favorite retail outlet.

Silhouette®
Where love comes alive™